# PROMISES TO KEEP

California Senator Eve Steele knew the issues, but when it came to the politics of loving, she lost all sense of diplomacy. Especially with her estranged husband, Alex, who could ruffle her cool image with a single fiery touch. Now Alex was running his own campaign—to win his wife back. He lured Eve into a passionate reunion, reigniting their smoldering love with kisses and caresses that made her forget everything—except that he still wanted a dedicated wife and a houseful of children and she wanted an office in the Capitol! Eve struggled to resist charming Alex, but she knew he'd be her toughest opponent ever. . . .

# PROMISES TO KEEP

*by*

*JoAnn Robb*

A SIGNET BOOK

NEW AMERICAN LIBRARY

## PUBLISHER'S NOTE

This novel is a work of fiction. Names, characters, places, and incidents either are the product of the author's imagination or are used fictitiously, and any resemblance to actual persons, living or dead, events, or locales is entirely coincidental.

NAL BOOKS ARE AVAILABLE AT QUANTITY DISCOUNTS
WHEN USED TO PROMOTE PRODUCTS OR SERVICES.
FOR INFORMATION PLEASE WRITE TO PREMIUM MARKETING DIVISION,
NEW AMERICAN LIBRARY, 1633 BROADWAY,
NEW YORK, NEW YORK 10019.

SIGNET, SIGNET CLASSIC, MENTOR, PLUME, MERIDIAN AND NAL BOOKS
are published by New American Library,
1633 Broadway, New York, New York 10019

First Printing, October, 1985

1 2 3 4 5 6 7 8 9

PRINTED IN THE UNITED STATES OF AMERICA

*To Jay, my husband, lover,*
*and best friend—my own Alex Steele*

# Chapter One

*"What the hell is this?"*

Eve Steele looked up in surprise as a folded newspaper was slapped onto her desk. Her eyes flew to the aggressive stance of the tall man in front of her.

"It looks like a newspaper," she quipped, making a half-hearted attempt at levity.

Whatever the problem, it was far too beautiful a day for tantrums. The Los Angeles sun, wonder of wonders, had valiantly managed to slice its way through the smog, splintering the sky with shafts of pure gold. The clarity of the early autumn day intensified the lush landscaping outside the garden suite of offices. Although air-conditioning precluded opening the windows, Eve imagined she could breathe in the piquant scent of the creeping rosemary that spilled from weathered tubs.

Like too many residents of the city, Eve would willingly have pleaded guilty to taking the weather for granted. It took days like this to make one stop and bask in the glow of California sunshine. But she was not to be allowed that luxury today. A well-manicured male hand flipped open the paper, jabbing a finger at the damning headline on the entertainment pages.

"Why didn't you tell me about this?"

Eve stared at him. In all their years of working together, she'd never seen Barry Matthews so angry. Her gaze lowered obediently to the bold thirty-six-point type. Alarm and confusion widened her hazel eyes as they focused on the words, and then she felt the blood drain from her face.

"I don't know . . . I mean, I didn't know anything about it," she stammered uncharacteristically as she met his glare.

"Well, what should we do now?" Barry folded his arms over the vest of his impeccably tailored gray suit. The look he was giving Eve was definitely accusing, and irritation at his attitude served to clear her head.

"*We* don't do anything," she replied crisply, rising from behind the desk and taking the newspaper with her. "You're staying here. But you can bet your last opinion poll that I'm going to wring someone's neck!"

Her flash of temper was in direct contrast with the peaceful surroundings of the office. Everything in the room spoke of money and good taste, from the soft plush of the muted blue carpeting and French provincial furnishings to the impressionist paintings on the blue walls. The owner of the quietly elegant office reflected the same image. At five feet four, Eve Steele had often wished for a few more inches, but her carriage and confident demeanor always gave the impression of height. Her slim figure never carried an ounce more or less than one hundred and ten pounds, the result of good genes inherited from a long line of slim ancestors, plus an almost addictive habit of daily exercise and an iron will at the table.

She marched to the door in long, angry strides, her plum silk dress swishing against her slender legs. The young woman seated at the reception desk in the outer office half rose from her chair at Eve's approach. She'd never seen her employer like this. If there was one thing Eve Meredith Steele was known for, it was her calm demeanor. Yet at this moment, she appeared to be breathing fire.

"Kim, I'll be gone the rest of the afternoon. Don't send any calls home; just take messages and I'll get back to everyone as soon as I can." If I'm not in jail for aggravated assault, Eve thought furiously.

"But Senator Steele, you've got that meeting with the Committee on Welfare Reform at three o'clock."

"Barry, you go," Eve flung over her shoulder without a moment's hesitation.

"But what will I tell them?"

She turned, trying to curb her frustration as she faced the astonished members of her staff. They were both looking at her as if she'd suddenly turned into a green monster. Something from one of Alex's movies. Alex. Damn that man!

"You legislative aides are renowned for your aptitude for prevarication, Barry. I haven't given you much opportunity to use that talent, but I'd suggest you try it today."

She slammed the door behind her, leaving a stunned, shared silence in the suite of offices.

"Well, you're home early." Eve was met at the front door by Mrs. Jacobs, her long-time housekeeper. The woman's usually stony face was wreathed in a large smile. "He's back."

"Don't I know it," Eve muttered. "The man made damn certain the entire world knew he was back."

She walked past Mrs. Jacobs, moving as fast as she could toward the master bedroom. Flinging open the louvered doors of the closet, Eve tensed when she saw the neatly arranged male clothing taking up half the racks. Moving to the dresser, her suspicions were further confirmed. Her lingerie had been moved, the top drawer once again filled with decidedly male briefs and socks. A quick perusal of the adjoining bathroom demonstrated the same evidence, as did a slight, musky aroma that lingered in the air. After all this time, Eve could recognize the unmistakable scent of her husband's after-shave like a blind kitten recognizes its mother. How dare he!

Her skirt swirled about her legs as she raced back down the long, curving stairway, marching into the dining room, where she found the object of her ire. He was eating an enormous roast turkey sandwich and drinking a cup of freshly brewed tea. Alex Steele had always been able to wrap women about his little finger, so why should her housekeeper be any different? The thought rankled. The woman had all the personality of the Sphinx, but she'd always been loyal—until now.

"What's the meaning of this?" Eve slammed the newspaper down with the same intensity with which Barry had flung it at her. "And what are your things doing in *my* room?"

Dark eyes that had been observing her stormy entrance dropped to the paper, and the corners of his lips quirked slightly, as if holding in a smile. He lifted his head back to watch her standing so furiously over him and his casual expression made Eve want to scream. Her life was crumbling all around her and all she could see in his eyes was amusement.

"My dear wife," Alex replied calmly, "as I recall, that delightfully decorated room upstairs is referred to as the master bedroom." He nodded in the direction of the now-crumpled black-and-white newsprint. "As you can clearly read, the master has come home."

Eve continued to glare at him, reining in the impulse to kick in the rear legs of the chair he was tilting back at a precarious angle. Some perverse instinct had her wishing to see that arrogantly posed body sprawled all over the terrazzo-tiled floor.

He hadn't changed. She didn't know why she ever expected that he might. After all, Alex had only been gone six months. Six very long months that had irrevocably altered her life, Eve reminded herself with a bitterness she thought she'd put behind her.

In a town where blonde was the norm, where men and women strove to achieve the image of sun-drenched beaches and convertibles with the tops down, Alex Steele stood out like a blizzard in July. His thick, wavy hair was as dark as anthracite coal. Premature streaks of silver graced his temples like blazing comets, adding not age but sophistication to the stark features of his face. Thick brows jutted over hooded eyes, like two inky caterpillars wearing their winter coats. A glint of mockery had stolen into those eyes, which were at this moment a dark chocolate brown. But they could turn into deep black wells at a moment's provocation or flame with unequaled passion. Eve had experienced both in their brief time together.

A straight, uncompromising nose directed her gaze to his mouth, the top lip shaded by a black mustache. His well-molded, thrusting chin showed not a sign of the bluish shadow that required shaving twice a day, and Eve knew her sense of smell had not misled her. He'd shaved recently. In *her* bathroom. His dark skin was smooth and fragrant with the heady aroma of musk.

Alex was silent, allowing her studied examination, his face absurdly bland. There was only the slightest flicker in his dark eyes that told her he was thoroughly enjoying himself—at her expense. Eve shrugged. So what else was new?

Her eyes traveled to his body, clad in a pair of jeans and a western shirt. The man was a study in contradictions, Eve thought, eyeing the combination. The jeans appeared to have been purchased off a rack in a store catering to real cowboys. Well washed and faded, they were just the proper width at the bottom of the leg to slide over his silvery lizard-skin boots. She knew, were he to stand and turn around, the only label on his rear would be a tough leather one.

The shirt, on the other hand, went beyond the fantasies of the most colorful urban cowboy. The detailed stitching indicated that it was handmade, and Eve knew that silk was not a material worn by men on the range. But Alex Steele had a weakness. He loved the stuff, and it wasn't a need to impress. "It just feels so damn good," he'd always said. In the same way that Alex Steele enjoyed good food and fine wine, he loved the cool sensation of silk against his skin. He'd filled Eve's closets with dresses of the sleek material, and she'd come to share his appreciation.

The clothes encased a figure that was as hard and lean as ever. An inch or so under six feet, Alex possessed an unshakable confidence and an air of command that allowed him to overshadow any other man who might be in the room with him. To women, the lambent sexuality and predatory force were far more compelling than mere good looks. I should know, Eve thought, having experienced it with life-shattering consequences. At the moment, he was imbued with a lazy insolence, taking over her home as if he possessed some divine right of kings. He showed no evidence of sharing the inner scars she bore. In fact, he looked better than ever.

"Everything where you remember it to be?" His low

voice taunted her softly, dark eyes dancing at her prolonged study.

"I hadn't expected you to lose anything," Eve replied acidly, stiffening at his teasing words. "After all, according to the columns, you've been far too busy giving it away to misplace it for long."

He arched a dark brow rakishly. "Ouch! Is that any way for a respectable state senator to speak? What would your constituency say?"

"What are you doing here, Alex?" she asked bluntly, in no mood to play games.

"I live here, remember?"

Eve shook her head. "No, you don't. And haven't for some time."

"I had a film to direct. Surely you read that in the papers. Did you think I'd just popped out for a pack of cigarettes and disappeared?"

"One can always hope."

He made an exaggerated wounded grimace in response to her words. "Don't get nasty, love. It's not your style. I've simply finished shooting my little epic and have returned to home and hearth, where I can put on my slippers and sit by the fire with my wife at my side and my faithful dog at my feet. Or is it my dog at my side and my faithful wife at my feet?" There was a quirk tilting his mouth under the black mustache.

Stung by his patent insincerity, Eve's rapid-fire mind skimmed through her range of options. She could give in to the temptation to break that crystal vase of fresh cut flowers over his head. That would bring immense satisfaction. But the man was so hard-headed, the only consequence would be that she'd be out one expensive Waterford vase.

She could call the police and have him thrown out, but

that would simply give birth to more headlines—something she certainly didn't need with a senatorial reelection campaign drawing to a close. There was no point in handing her opponent, Peter Jordan, ammunition like that.

She could telephone the head of Olympus Studios, demanding that their golden-touch director be shipped off to Timbuktu to film some desert saga, but her father had never been very cooperative in her dealings with Alex Steele. Why should he change now? It seemed that a daughter was an expendable asset, whereas a surefire hit director was worth his weight in gold. Eve knew where Jason Meredith's sympathies lay, and they weren't with her.

She could resort to the feminine ploy of tears, swallowing her immense pride and pleading with him to leave her alone, but Eve was no actress. He'd spot her amateur performance before she'd reached the hand-wringing. Then, after handing her a blistering review, he'd remain precisely where he was.

The only alternative left, Eve realized, was to summon forth her composure and make an attempt to discuss this like reasonable, intelligent adults.

She sat down, crossing her long legs in a fluid motion, the soft rustle of the silk breaking the expectant silence.

"Alex, how long do you plan on staying here?"

"Didn't you read past that headline? I've taken a sabbatical, sweetheart. I've no intention of taking on another project until after Election Day. Other candidates have wives to brighten up the long, wearisome campaign trail. You'll have your husband, Senator Steele."

Eve experienced a grim sense of foreboding. Whatever the man was up to, she didn't think he was kidding about this.

"May I ask when you came to this momentous decision?"

"I don't understand. You're my wife. I had to be away and now I'm home again. There wasn't any actual decision. It's simply the natural way."

Despite the turbulent emotion swirling around them, Alex was able to view this reunion scene with a director's detached viewpoint. He knew he was going to have to give the performance of his life and only hoped he could pull it off. She was as beautiful as ever. But more than that, when she'd marched into the room, she'd affected him like a jolt of sulfurous lightning—as she always had. He wasn't about to let Eve out of his life. He held firm, his dark eyes displaying a hard, assured gleam.

Eve realized belatedly what was wrong with her tactic. In order to discuss anything logically, it was preferable to have two rational people contributing to the dialogue, and Alex was refusing to cooperate.

"We're separated, Alex. Papers and everything. You *can* read, can't you? I had them delivered to your office in London."

A brief spark of anger flared in his dark eyes. "I can read. But those ridiculous papers were obviously the act of a hysterical, vindictive female. Whatever differences we may have had, Eve, I've always given you credit for being far more intelligent than that. So, I allowed you that little temper tantrum. Now I've returned home in order to provide you the opportunity to bring this grandstand play to a halt."

"Grandstand play?" Her hazel eyes widened to huge, tawny circles. "You can't believe I'm going to let you come back here as if nothing had happened in Mexico? As if anything could ever be the same between us?"

Alex dropped the chair back down onto all four legs. His

face was a carefully set mask of inscrutability, but his voice, when he decided to speak, was oddly rough.

"I'd say we both have some things to answer for as far as Mexico's concerned, but this isn't the time. I've brought you a present."

Eve watched as he rose with a lithe grace, moving to the glass table behind them. She tried to discern the meaning of his vague accusation, but it was beyond her. She was the wronged party; what was he doing acting as though he'd been injured by the fiasco?

Her mind flew back to that horrible weekend she'd spent in Mexico. She had expected her unplanned pregnancy to come as a shock to Alex. It had certainly surprised her as she faced a reelection campaign that would take an enormous amount of energy. But the mental image of a dark-eyed baby with thick black hair had been so appealing, and she had loved Alex so, that to give him a child was surely the most wonderful present she could imagine. She flew to Mexico, renting a car to take her to the remote Chihuahua location.

Eve had been shocked to discover that Alex expected her to give up her work as soon as her term in office expired. He had used the baby as an excuse to plan her life to his liking, using it as proof that she had no business continuing with her campaign. They had spent the weekend in the hot, shabby motel room, angry words flung back and forth on both sides.

Back home, Eve had thought her illness was nothing but a delayed reaction to the foreign water. But then she grew steadily weaker and had ended up in the hospital, her body infused with a rampant infection that had cost her their child.

Eve didn't hate Alex for not welcoming her on location. With the twenty-twenty vision of hindsight, she knew she should have known better than to drop in unannounced on a director working on a tight schedule.

She didn't hate him for his furious assertion that she had no business continuing to work, either. They'd never discussed it in their brief, whirlwind courtship, and although it had been a major bone of contention, Eve believed if they'd worked hard enough, they could have reached a compromise.

No, the reason she hated Alex Steele was his blatant indifference to the loss of their baby. He'd remained in Mexico, heartbreakingly silent. Then, as soon as the film had been sent to the studio for editing, he was off to London to direct the multi-million-dollar remake of *Wuthering Heights*. His behavior demonstrated all too clearly that he considered their marriage the mistake he'd declared it to be during their heated argument. Eve had begun the paperwork necessary to legally dissolve her already dead marriage.

''I think you'll like this.''

His voice broke into her troubled thoughts, and Eve focused her mind back on the present, watching as he took a pair of silver tongs and placed ice from the bucket into a crystal decanter. He poured some clear liquid over the ice, then reached into a small refrigerator and pulled out two chilled glasses, pouring the liquid from the decanter into the glasses, not allowing the ice to follow. He handed one to Eve, rocking back and forth on his heels to watch as she inhaled the delicate bouquet.

She lifted her eyebrows questioningly. ''Peaches?''

Alex nodded his head with a great deal of self-satisfaction. ''I brought it back from Europe. It's impossible to find a good peach brandy in this country. I knew you'd like it. Peach *was* your favorite kind, wasn't it?''

Eve wasn't going to let him undermine her defenses this

early in the day. She glanced down at her watch: three-thirty. She sighed, wondering briefly how Barry was doing, covering for her. He was out there lying to the voters while she sat in her dining room, trying to make polite conversation while sipping an expensive, imported fruit brandy. What would the welfare reform committee think of that?

"It's a little early, Alex." She put the glass down onto the table.

"Not in London," he argued, holding it out to her once again. "Since I'm still on London time and you're on California time, let's compromise. It's the cocktail hour in Peoria. Drink up, Eve."

The sweet aroma of the peach drifted up from the well-chilled glass, circling her head in a fragrant cloud, enticing her lips toward the crystal rim. She gave in to the dual enticements and took a tentative sip, allowing the taste to linger, a velvet cling of fruit on her tongue. Fired with the essence of orchards and the well-defined flavor of the soft peach, the experience was one of sheer bliss. Eve closed her eyes briefly, allowing the taste and bouquet to linger. She opened them to see Alex gazing in watchful concentration. He'd returned to the chair, tilting it back again. The exquisite taste returned her to the early days of their marriage and she momentarily put aside her anger. He'd always been able to soothe away her irritation with him, reaching into his sensual bag of tricks for a surefire diversion.

"It's heavenly," she admitted, a slight smile curving her lips.

Alex returned the smile, taking his first taste. Eve found her gaze following the glass to his lips, experiencing a shock of something that uncomfortably resembled desire forking through her as she remembered the taste and feel of those lips on hers.

"Just as good as I was promised," he agreed, his dark eyes glowing. At her, Eve wondered, or the brandy? His crooked grin tugged at something deep inside her and she had to struggle to maintain her composure. "I thought about tossing it in the door ahead of me, but I was afraid you'd whack me over the head with the bottle before we had a chance to try it out."

His grin grew bolder, encouraging her to join in the light mood, and Eve lowered her eyes to her glass, unable to answer with the scathing retort she knew he deserved. She took another long sip of the velvety fruit liqueur, blaming it for the warm flush racing through her blood.

Alex had introduced her to the *eaux de vie* on their honeymoon trip to France. One of the highlights had been dinner at an intimate little restaurant in Alsace, where they were invited into a small salon and served a variety of the sweet brandies. In truth, Alex Steele had introduced her to an entire world of sensuality, from the smooth, satiny wines, to the cling of cool silk against her bare skin, to the potent allure of his lovemaking. He'd awakened in her a hunger she'd never known existed and when he'd cajoled, urged, and stroked it to a primitive, clamoring pitch, he'd taught her the mindless bliss of shared possession.

To the outside world, the home in which Eve had spent her late teen years and early twenties seemed like Xanadu recreated in Beverly Hills. But in reality, all the luxuries that had surrounded her were simply a means of keeping score. Her father was a workaholic who had brought a struggling film studio to the zenith of power. The comforts he bought with the proceeds were his way of measuring success. A box-office smash might bring in a tennis court, a Picasso for the dining room wall, or a pair of miniature horses. They were chips in the constant gambling world of filmmaking in which her father lived and worked, nothing more.

The majority of Eve's youth had been spent in a Swiss boarding school. The German-trained nuns had never been known for their excesses, unless it might be an addiction to strong self-discipline. That had been encouraged in Eve by the use of a painful switch and long hours kneeling on the stone floors of the ancient chapel. She wore it now like a second skin. Except with Alex. Her self-restraint just flew out the window whenever she was around the man.

Oh, Alex had taught her sensuality, all right, Eve thought bitterly, her hands cupped around the crystal glass. The only problem was, he'd also taught her the depths of pain and suffering a person could endure and still survive.

Her thoughts returned once more to the present, and, just as she was almost falling under his dark, enticing spell once again, a slim vestige of self-protection returned to save her.

"I suppose it was you who called the press," she said.

"Of course."

"Of course," she agreed. "You've never given a moment's thought to my feelings, so why should this time be any different?" There was a barb in her smooth tones and Alex's dark eyes narrowed.

"That's a double-edged sword, Eve. If I were you, I'd handle it very carefully."

His low warning was issued with a gritty aggravation that Eve couldn't understand. Why in the world did he keep hinting that she had caused him grief? All she'd done was make the horrendous mistake of loving this man.

"I have no idea what you're talking about," she returned with feigned indifference.

"I'm home, Eve. Let's begin with that."

"It's over, Alex. It ended in Mexico." Eve's hazel eyes were as sharp as a well-honed razor, daring him to deny the treacherous words he had thrown at her in the heat of their battle in that tacky motel room.

"Mexico was a mistake," he surprised her by saying. "We both said things we shouldn't have, things we didn't mean. And despite everything, you're the only woman in my life, Eve. The only woman I've ever wanted in my life."

Eve arched a delicate eyebrow. "Are you telling me that all the stories of you spreading your gospel of self-indulgence over Europe in the past six months are lies, *darling?"* She invested the endearment, which was thrown about all too casually in this town, with heavy irony.

As Eve watched his eyes grow darker, irises merging with pupils, she felt a modicum of satisfaction. She'd obviously gotten him with that one. She might not be able to hurt him like he'd hurt her, but at least she'd pierced his armor and proven him vulnerable.

"I could prove it to you," Alex murmured.

"And just how would you do that?"

He was standing over her before she heard the front legs of the chair hit the tile floor. Before she could raise one hand in protest, or defense, he'd hauled her to him. Effectively trapped between the unyielding teak dining room table and the equally hard male body, Eve fought against responding to the gleam in his dark gaze.

"No, Alex, it's over," she whispered, knowing her soft denial was no honest protest. God help her, it had been so very, very long since his strong arms had held her this way.

"Prove it to me then, Eve . . . I've waited long enough for you to come to your senses. Go ahead, show me that I'm the only one who's been going crazy over this bloody separation."

# Chapter Two

Eve was stunned to find herself face to face with an entirely different Alex Steele than the one who'd brought her the exquisite fruit brandy. This man appeared relentless and implacable. Heathcliff, she realized. Caught up in the creative tyranny of directing, Alex had somehow absorbed the dark, brooding, intensely destructive nature of the fierce antihero.

She watched, mesmerized, as his dark head lowered, his eyes open as they searched hers, probing for hidden secrets. Eve's murmured protest was swallowed by his mouth covering hers with a persuasion that allowed no rebuttal. Her hands pushed against his shoulders, offering token resistance, but Alex shook his head as he captured her wrists in one strong hand, holding them harmless behind her back.

The movement arched her body upward, pressing her closer to him, and her head twisted as she tried to ignore the long-slumbering passions that were clamoring to be heard. Alex's free hand grasped the back of her honey-blonde head, holding her to the kiss, but even then it could only be considered a tender assault he was waging on her senses.

Eve's mouth opened for a moment, seeking life-sustaining air and, as he filled the dark cavern with his tongue, the forgotten crystal glass dropped from her fingers to the floor, shattering with an ear-splitting sound they both ignored.

His free hand moved down her back as he widened his spread-legged stance and pulled her intimately into the cradle of his thighs. The sumptuous Italian silk of her dress sighed in concert with his shirt as their bodies moved against each other and Eve could feel her traitorous nipples gathering themselves into expectant little points, stimulated by the caress. There were no words, no soft sighs of pleasure nor whispered moans of desire. Just the rustling of the material as his roving hands augmented his message of primal intent. His firm mouth plucked at the softness of her lips, coaxing surrender.

Eve fought the weakness permeating her rebellious body as it responded with remembered ecstasy to his clever hands. She reminded herself that he had no right. He was the one who'd ruined everything. Even as she fought for strength, her head swam with suppressed need.

Alex's lips moved up her cheekbone, feathering light kisses as delicate as dandelion fluff upon her blazing skin. His dark eyes smoldered with a hungry fire as they stared down into her confused gaze and his lips brushed her lids, encouraging her to close her eyes. Those lips were everywhere, tracing stinging little paths over her face and down her neck, plucking gently at her skin, urging her to give up the battle and join with him in the victory celebration.

Alex released her hands when he felt the tell-tale tremor of her body against his, revealing that he no longer had to hold her to the close embrace. No, what he was using as a weapon was far more deadly, Eve realized. His fingers moved to undo the first two buttons of her shirtwaist dress, then his hot lips lowered to the pulse spot in her throat, as if drawing her life's blood through her pores. The kiss had a crazy effect on her equilibrium and she held his shoulders for support.

Alex's lips burned her skin in the vee created by the open buttons, but he made no gesture to continue. His hands traveled up and down her curves, skimming past her breasts. Those hands roving so near, yet not moving to embrace the soft, thrusting curves, made her tingle all the more with desire and she could think of nothing but the need for his touch.

Her skin was on fire, flames coursing under the cool plum silk, and all Eve could do was press against him, molding her curves to his rigid male form. If Alex wouldn't do anything about this burning need, she'd have to, she realized, unable to take any more of his sweet torture.

Her fingers moved to his chest, unbuttoning his indigo shirt so she could slide her palms against his warm, moist skin. Her fingers danced enticingly, curling in the thick black hair on his chest before sliding around to feather the rippling muscles of his back. Eve gave in to the overwhelming urge to press her lips to the fragrant skin while her body rubbed against him, like a purring kitten asking to be petted.

When Alex finally broke the silence, his voice was rough with unmistakable desire. "Tell me what you want," he commanded, his warm breath heating her ear. "You have to tell me, Eve."

"Oh, Alex."

Eve trembled, her entire body quaking with desire. She knew at this moment she'd register at least a ten on her personal Richter scale. It had been so long! Alex had taught her, during their brief, tempestuous marriage, to relate her desires with both words and actions, but now the words were sticking in her throat.

There was something so damning about saying such things aloud. It put the responsibility right where it belonged, on her own shoulders. Eve wanted him to take charge. She didn't want to think herself capable of such hunger.

"Tell me," he repeated with a soft insistence.

"Touch me . . . please, Alex?" It was a barely discernible whisper, but it seemed to satisfy him.

He unbuttoned the remainder of the pearl buttons to her waist, allowing his hands to cup her love-swelled breasts in his palms. Lowering his ebony head, his lips dampened the sloping softness above the lacy bra. Eve drew in her breath as one long, teasing finger insinuated itself into the top of the lace-trimmed cup, following the outline, tantalizing her to a spiraling agony. She could feel her nipples hardening to tiny rubies just below his touch, but still he slowed even more, seemingly determined to take his time.

"Alex . . . Please . . ." Her eyes pleaded with him. "Kiss me." The last was added on a hoarse gasp as his left hand moved to draw her lower body into his, allowing her to share his arousal.

Alex granted her request, deftly undoing the front clasp of the bra before his palms lifted the soft warmth to his lips. He caressed her breasts with his tongue until they were damp and burning, then he raised his head, his gaze clashing with Eve's.

"So soft," he murmured. "It's hard to tell where the silk leaves off and the satin of your skin starts." His dark fingers lightly stroked her flesh. "But you're much, much softer, Eve."

Eve felt consumed by his glowing black eyes, unable to

look away as his desire scorched itself into her brain. Then his mouth curved in a knowing, masculine smile, and his head lowered once again, his lips curling around the hard buds. The jet mustache brushed teasingly against her skin as his teeth tugged tenderly, drawing warmth from her very core.

The silk rustled under their undulating movements and Eve felt certain Alex was prepared to take her right there, pressed against the teak dining room table. And despite her earlier vow, she knew she'd help him. She was on the verge of losing her last vestige of coherent thought when the chiming of the doorbell broke into the heavy sound of their breathing. Brought back to reality with a jolt, she pushed against his chest with a frantic pressure.

"Alex, stop. Stop!"

He stepped back from her flailing hands, heaving with deep gulping breaths as he looked at her with frustrated astonishment.

"You can't expect me to stop now?" he asked, a hoarse note of disbelief in his voice.

"I do— You must— Someone's—" The words fell out pell-mell, a note of faint hysteria edging the usually well-modulated tones.

"Mrs. Steele?" There was a discreet knock on the dining room door and Eve gathered the front of her dress together in trembling hands as she answered on an unsteady breath.

"Yes, Mrs. Jacobs. I'll be right there."

Her housekeeper had the foresight not to come in, Eve noted, thinking irrationally that both Alex and her father would laugh at her for being embarrassed in front of the help.

"It's Mr. Matthews, Mrs. Steele. I suggested he wait for you on the terrace."

"Thank you." Eve's fingers had turned to stone as she fumbled ineffectively with the tiny buttons.

"Here, let me help." Alex's breathing had returned to normal, and his deep voice was controlled.

She wanted to jerk away from him, but he was already maneuvering the gleaming white pearls through the silk loops. His palms skimmed her body, pulling her skirt back down over her hips. Then he squatted down to gather up the scattered hairpins from the tile floor, picking them carefully out of the shards of broken crystal. Holding them out to her, his mouth lifted at the corners in an intimate, satisfied smile.

"I rest my case," he murmured as he watched her shaking fingers attempt to make some semblance of order in what had earlier been a sleek, sophisticated twist at the back of her neck.

Eve looked up, her eyes bleak. She didn't know exactly how he'd done it, caused her to respond like that. Like Pavlov's dog being offered a big bowl of Alpo. She no longer loved him; she'd firmly convinced herself of that these past months. Yet, Alex Steele had succeeded in making her beg. She felt like the hairpins they'd both ground under their feet.

"What?" she asked, after a long, miserable silence.

"If I hadn't been celibate all these long, lonely months, I would have been able to wait until we retired to that comfortable king-sized bed upstairs. Even at our most lustful," he grinned, devilish lights dancing in the dark eyes, "I don't remember ravishing you on this table. It's bound to be as hard as the tile floor. I think we can do better, sweetheart."

Eve turned away from his provocative glance, studying her reflection in the beveled glass wall mirror. Damning evidence was written all over her. Her dress was creased as if she'd slept in it, her dark blonde hair was only precariously restrained into order, her lips were bruised and swollen and her face—well, she might as well be wearing a neon sign on her downcast features, she thought in disgust.

She experienced a jolt as her eyes lifted slightly to meet Alex's in the mirror. She might be hating her disheveled appearance, but his gaze was definitely appreciative.

"You're lovely." His low words echoed the gleam in his eyes and Eve jerked her gaze away, returning to her critical appraisal. In doing so, she missed the warm mixture of compassion and wonder that darkened his eyes as Alex pondered how right she felt in his arms, how right she fit into his life. He only hoped he could make her love him again . . . in time.

Eve's face was flushed and hot, her impeccably applied makeup having been either kissed or burned off. Her anguish was mirrored in the hazel depths of her eyes and her shoulders drooped in defeat. What in the world would Barry think? Her dismay at having to appear like this before her long-time friend and associate was only slightly eased by the excuse to escape Alex's unblinking study.

As she warily lifted her eyes again to his in the mirror, he was watching her with the intensity of a natural predator. As he caught her appraisal, Alex's gaze suddenly turned unfathomable, no longer sparked with the glow of male appreciation. Moving without her usual self-confident step, Eve felt like a frightened crab scuttling away in the sand.

Barry's attitude was as studiously proper as the charcoal pinstripe suit he wore. He greeted Eve casually, refraining from any comments on her appearance. But, as his keen eyes made a swift inventory, she knew he hadn't missed a thing.

"Barry. I hadn't expected to see you this afternoon."

Eve sought to keep the censure from her voice. He had, in a manner of speaking, rescued her. But she'd also made it clear that she expected no calls to be relayed home. Surely Barry had understood that to mean she wanted to be alone with Alex while she discovered what he was up to.

"I just dropped by to report on the meeting," he answered. Then he sank into a cushioned wicker chair, raking his fingers through his blonde hair. "Oh hell, Eve. To be honest, I felt it was my duty, as your friend, to check in and see what your estranged spouse is up to these days. Any more little surprises like that one and you might as well kiss your reelection chances goodbye."

Eve settled herself into one of the chairs across from him, extending her arms along the length of the white wicker.

"I don't know, Barry," she hedged. "I'd think a married woman, with a husband living at home, would be far more acceptable to the voters than a woman in the midst of an expensive, messy divorce proceeding. Hypothetically speaking, of course," she added in qualification.

Intense gray eyes narrowed as they surveyed her calm demeanor. "Are we speaking hypothetically, Eve?"

"Tell me about the meeting," she instructed, very much in command again as she detoured the conversation away from her marriage and Alex. She'd successfully changed from a distressed, flustered woman to the brisk and businesslike state senator.

There was a flash of irritation in his analytical gaze, but Eve maintained her poise, smiling encouragingly for him to relate the outcome of the meeting she'd ducked. Barry sighed, crossing his legs as he leaned back in the chair. Only the pewter-toned Gucci loafer, swinging as he spoke, displayed his irritation. Barry's face had settled into its correct, politician's mask, Eve noted, something he could slide on and off at will.

Can't we all? she admitted mentally. Although it was a learned skill, she'd always considered it an innate talent. Those who weren't born with the ability seemed incapable of survival in the goldfish-bowl existence of the political arena.

Barry braced his elbows on the arm of the chair, making a little tent with his fingertips. "It went very well. I think Harris is swinging over to our side, which would ensure the labor vote again. And that never hurts."

"Especially since the reform measures would benefit everyone. Including labor," Eve reminded him pointedly. "What little excuse did you think up for my absence?"

A smile warmed his handsome face, showing a wide crescent of straight white teeth. "I explained you'd received an unexpected summons from the governor's aide concerning the highway-use taxation. Since that will affect everyone's pocketbook, they were willing to play second fiddle, especially since it was Al Harrison who'd bumped them."

She watched him critically, a small frown marring the smooth skin between her brows. She had, she reminded herself, told him to lie—but it still left her feeling uncomfortable.

"Barry, wasn't that unwise? If it leaks out, how do we explain that I haven't been anywhere near the state offices since the end of the session?"

The man's tanned features remained under smooth control. "No problem. Harrison is in town for a few days. I called him at Las Casitas on Catalina, where he's soaking up some sun and playing a few rounds of golf. He's got us covered."

Eve didn't like to ponder just what Barry Matthews knew that had made one of the governor's top aides fall into line so easily. Sometimes Barry worried her. There was a tacit conspiracy of silence in the old-time political ranks, but everyone who played the game knew just who held the winning hand and who didn't. Barry Matthews had never walked away from a table a loser in his life.

He had orchestrated some of the most successful campaigns in the state, and Eve had been floored, six years before, when he'd shown up at her campaign office, offering to fill the key slot on her staff. She'd been a political neophyte then, not usually worthy of notice by the big boys in power, despite her father's vast fortune. A maverick from the word go, Jason Meredith eschewed the necessary compromises essential in politics. But Barry had spotted something in her, he'd explained at the time. He knew they could go all the way together.

"All the way?" she'd asked blankly, not having looked past that initial campaign for the state senate.

"All the way," he'd repeated with a certain calm authority. "Governor's mansion, Washington—whatever we want."

They worked well together, despite the fact that some dissenters described Barry Matthews as a hired shark, always on the lookout for political blood. Eve privately felt he was too handsome, too cultivated for that label. A Venus's flytrap, she considered, eyeing him now. Pretty and alluring, and probably deadly.

"Sometimes I wonder why *you* don't run for office," Eve said her thoughts aloud. "You're articulate, well-respected in the party, handsome." She gave him a brilliant smile. "All the women would vote for you without your even having to open your mouth."

He laughed disarmingly. "I prefer working at the edges of the limelight's glow, behind the scenes."

"Ah yes," Eve nodded, her smile widening. "The king-maker."

"Queen-maker," Barry corrected easily, gray eyes flashing with shared humor.

Eve began to relax. Barry was good for her. He knew how to get her elected, how to pull the right strings to get an important bill through a committee. And, what was important right now, he knew how to make her laugh.

"The power behind the throne," she continued the playful analogies.

"As long as he isn't auditioning to be the man behind a certain successful woman," a deep voice drawled laconically. "That part's already been cast."

Two pairs of startled eyes flew immediately to the source. Alex lounged in the doorway, his shoulders against the frame, his hands thrust deeply into the pockets of his faded jeans. The motion drew the material snugly against his lean body and Eve noted the blue denim was almost white where it rubbed against his thighs. He'd failed to rebutton the royal blue silk shirt, and her cheeks burned as she took in the raised welts scoring his dark chest. She'd left those there, and he was wearing them as a warning to Barry Matthews—a warning to stay away from his wife. The nerve!

Barry was too consummate a politician to reveal any reaction to those scarlet welts as he responded to Alex's thinly veiled challenge.

"Well, well, the prodigal returns." He put a wealth of sarcasm into his well-modulated voice, sliding a glance over to Eve. "Are you inviting me to dinner, boss lady? I've always enjoyed dining on fatted calf."

Barry was baiting Alex with all the slick tools he'd

acquired over the years, Eve realized with surprise, but she didn't know exactly why. It was a dangerous game, one she wasn't sure even Barry could survive unscathed. Yet, to her astonishment, Alex chose to let the taunting jibe pass in silence. He moved instead to her side, settling himself onto the arm of her chair. The wicker creaked in protest, but Alex remained where he was, running his fingers lightly over her shoulder blades in a familiar, possessive gesture.

"Sorry," he said finally, giving Barry an artificial smile, "but my wife and I are planning an intimate little supper this evening. I'm sure you understand, Matthews."

"Of course," Barry returned with equally insincere politeness, nodding his blonde head. He rose from the chair, sliding his hand into the pocket of his gray slacks, a gesture that pushed back his superbly cut jacket. Barry was well over six feet two, yet Eve knew that, should Alex stand beside her legislative aide, some masculine optical illusion would take place, dwarfing Barry's superior height and arrogantly controlled posture.

If Barry was described as a Greek god, a term she'd heard the senate secretaries use, Alex was the flip side of the coin. Lucifer—the most enticing and deadly of all the fallen angels.

"You are planning to keep to your appearance schedule tomorrow, aren't you, Eve? I've booked the entire day and I'd hate to see you miss the exposure." Barry glared briefly at Alex. "Just as I'd hate to see any personal problems endanger the campaign at this late date."

It had taken a tremendous effort on Eve's part to put herself back together and begin this campaign. Whatever limited role she allowed him in her personal life, Barry's words were obviously chosen to remind both Eve and her estranged husband that Barry was in charge of her career.

His gray eyes were cold as they slashed a warning Alex's way.

"I'll be ready at seven, on the dot," she agreed swiftly, before Alex could interject a response. "Shall I meet you at the office?"

Barry looked at the dark man who had just covered Eve's slim hand with his own. "No," he decided, "I'll pick you up. Since we'll be working so closely all day, it'll be simpler if we only use one car. That way I've got you all to myself between stops." He rocked back a bit on his heels, having thrown the gauntlet down. While his words pertained only to business, the implication lacing the smooth words was that he and Eve had an overly close relationship. This time, Alex couldn't ignore it, she knew.

But, to her astonishment, Alex let it pass as well. The placid look on his chiseled features would have been the envy of any political warhorse.

"Well," Alex's deep voice broke the little pool of expectant silence, "if you're all finished, Matthews, I'll call Mrs. Jacobs to see you out."

Barry gave him a smile which didn't begin to reach the silvery eyes. "Don't bother, Steele. I know my way around Eve's house. I've been coming here for years."

Eve smothered a gasp of disbelief. This verbal battle had taken a decidedly personal twist. She wanted to call a halt to it, but didn't want to be drawn into the fray directly—this was suddenly out of her league.

Alex's impenetrable face didn't respond to Barry's latest challenge, but Eve felt the pressure of his fingers as they tightened with concealed emotion over hers.

"Then I'd suggest you do that," Alex murmured with that dangerous, satiny tone she'd learned to recognize. "My wife and I have a great deal of catching up to do."

"Eve?" Gray eyes met hers, questioning whether she wanted—or needed—him to remain.

"Goodbye, Barry," she said softly. "I'll see you first thing in the morning.

Eve watched him walk away, wishing she could go with him. She wasn't looking forward to being alone again with Alex.

"You could have buttoned your shirt," she hissed up at him as Barry left the terrace.

A smile ruffled his mouth under the black mustache. "It's my home, too," he reminded her. "It seems to me that if I choose to leave my shirt unbuttoned, or wander around the privacy of my own domicile in my underwear—or nothing at all—it's Matthews's problem if he's offended. I don't remember inviting him here. As it was, he picked one helluva time to drop in."

"Barry Matthews has *never* needed an invitation to this house!"

Alex rose from the arm of the chair, his mask slipping to reveal a hard-bitten set to his features. Dark eyes glistened with ominous warning, like a thundercloud moving across the sun. He'd avoided a direct confrontation, knowing it would only lessen his chances, but Alex could no longer hold back his resentment that Barry Matthews had apparently usurped his position in Eve's life.

"He does from now on." Alex hated himself the moment he heard the words escape uncensored from his lips. Damn. What was it about Eve that made him respond like a storm trooper whenever they fell into one of these discussions?

He had nothing against women's liberation. Not in theory, at any rate. It was only when Eve got her back up and insisted on being so damned independent that he wanted to strangle her.

He'd managed to make a great deal of money in his life, yet it had never really meant anything to him until he'd walked into that party nine months ago and met the woman of his dreams. Finally the rewards of his lifelong labors had a purpose—he wanted to spend every last cent making Eve Meredith Steele's life a paradise on earth.

But she'd maintained the ridiculous notion that she wanted to remain self-supporting. While she accepted his extravagant gifts, she had insisted on maintaining her home and career; combined with the demands of his own work it had kept them from having anything but a marriage of fleeting acquaintance. Alex's irritation at this entire situation flared once again, and he decided to leave the terrace before he said something else he'd regret.

Eve glared at his silk-clad back as Alex marched from the terrace, the heels of his boots tapping on the flagstone. She sighed deeply, turning to watch the play of sunlight on the sparkling water of the swimming pool, deciding irrationally that she hated Daylight Savings Time. Someone should pass a resolution repealing it; she needed an extra hour to this day like she needed a plague of locusts. It was hard enough facing down the man, but trying to do it in the golden California sun made it worse. Every strained line on her face showed. Once the sun had dipped into the vast Pacific, she would at least be able to hide her expression in the dim shadows of evening.

Ha! Eve attacked herself furiously, recrossing her long legs with a vicious gesture. She couldn't even handle her emotions when she was alone with Alex at three-thirty in the afternoon. If she didn't force some steel into her weak spine, she'd be a goner come nightfall. To sleep with him once again in that large, lonely bed—

Eve pressed her fingertips against her temples. This simply had to stop! The bed. That was the place to start.

Eliminate the gravest danger. She rose with renewed determination and climbed the stairs to the bedroom, where she began yanking things from the closet.

Alex poured two fingers of scotch into a glass, then, reconsidering, filled the short, stout glass to the brim. Throwing his head back, he tossed off the liquor in long thirsty gulps. Vowing that this time he would not give up so easily, he returned to the terrace, only to find it deserted.

A short search located Eve in their bedroom, her actions proving that he was definitely in for an uphill battle. Taking a deep breath, Alex garnered strength to begin again.

# Chapter Three

"What are you doing?"

"What does it look like? I'm moving my things out of the *master's* bedroom."

Alex was by her side in two swift strides, taking the dress from her hands. "I don't remember evicting you," he said softly.

"That's funny," Eve answered, reaching for the flame silk chiffon dinner dress, "because I most definitely remember evicting you. For all the good it's done."

"Eve—" His voice held an almost appealing quality and she lifted wary hazel eyes to his face, hardening her heart to what she was afraid she'd find there. But his expression had grown remote.

"Yes?"

Alex shrugged, unwilling to reveal how desperately he wanted to take her to bed here and now. While they'd never solved any of their problems that way, it had put an end to one helluva lot of arguments, he thought. But in those days she hadn't been so willing to deny her body pleasure in order to win a point. No, this definitely wasn't going to be easy.

"Do whatever you want," he replied, managing a bland tone.

He flopped down onto the oriental bedspread, watching her silently. Eve felt unnerved by his mute, intense study as she moved to the dresser, taking out the filmy items of French lingerie he'd purchased for her trousseau while they were in Europe. Little bits of lace and satin and silk, the items were designed to give pleasure to the wearer and the observer.

"Do you mind?" Her defensive eyes shot daggers at the man lying so imperially on the bed. She meant for him to leave, but was not surprised when he opted to misunderstand.

"Of course I do," Alex replied quietly. "Any man would mind if his wife moved out of their bedroom." He picked up a peach chiffon teddy, fingering the lacy insert absently. "But, I can wait, I suppose."

Eve grabbed the teddy back and put it with the pile she'd created at the foot of the bed. "If you're waiting for me, Alex, don't bother. It won't happen."

"You're my wife. I'm old-fashioned enough to believe it's preferable for a married couple to sleep in the same bed. Whenever possible."

"I won't be your wife for long, Alex. Our court date has been set."

"I understand that. But I don't understand why you're so intent on political suicide. I've already informed the press of our blissful reconciliation. How will it look if you kick me out? Everyone accepts a little marital spat with newlyweds, sweetheart, but this constant vacillating on your part will look as though you're unfit for public office."

His dark eyes danced with barely suppressed humor. "Isn't there an old saw about women politicians being too emotional? Something to do with hormonal swings? I think you're stuck with me, love. Until the election, anyway."

Eve stared at him, her mouth dry as a huge lump grew in her throat. The thought had been weaving a little web of fear and doubt in her mind since those words had first leaped off the newspaper page at her. He'd managed to back her into a very tight corner and there didn't appear to be a graceful way out. The only thing she didn't understand was why he had done it.

There were those, Barry included, who would argue that Alex wanted to keep her as his wife to maintain his position at Olympus Studios. But Eve was no fool when it came to the film industry. She knew her father would never let anyone's personal life interfere in a business decision; not even hers. Profit was always first and foremost with the man.

Add to that the fact that in reality, Olympus Studios needed Alex far more than the director needed them, and that argument turned into so much tapioca pudding. Olympus, like every other major Hollywood film studio, had undergone a period of change, no longer making a hundred pictures a year. Instead, they were producing ten or so, and since most of the pictures were financial failures, there were only a handful of what were referred to as "bankable directors," those who could be counted on to come up with a blockbuster. One hit movie could move a studio from the red into the black instantly, and Alex Steele was the ace up the sleeve of Olympus Studios.

One big smash like *The Zenith Probe* could pay the bills for a long time. No, Alex was not suddenly fighting this divorce in order to hold on to his career. His career had taken off like a rocket with *The Star Seekers* years ago and it had shown not a single sign of slowing as it soared like a blazing comet past more established Hollywood names. So, why did he even care?

"What do you want?" Eve's sophistication dropped away for an instant, revealing an aura of fragility that she was unaware of.

Alex's gaze fixed on her face before sweeping over the rest of her, his look long and level. "The same thing I've wanted since the moment I walked into that party, Eve. I want you."

How could she ever forget? The dark, diabolically compelling man who had walked up to her, taken her hand, held her gaze to his and declared, "I don't have any idea who you are, but I intend to have you. Permanently."

Eve scooped up a handful of clothing and moved toward the door, pausing to fling an answer back over her shoulder. "You've got about as much chance for that, Alex Steele, as an ice cube in hell."

She marched down the hallway, putting her clothing into one of the guest rooms. Something was going to have to be done about him, she realized, it would just take a while to think up a plan. Eve was an intelligent woman; she'd devise something.

"Beautiful." Alex's eyes paid compliments as Eve entered the dining room two hours later. He took in her slim crimson slacks and matching blouse. "A flame. But red is a rather aggressive choice, wouldn't you say? I was hoping for something a little softer. Frillier."

"I don't dress for you, Alex." She accepted the glass of dark burgundy he was offering.

"I know, love. And I much prefer it when you *don't* dress for me."

Eve cringed at the double entendre. "Knock it off, Alex. It won't work."

A pitch-black eyebrow arched rakishly. "What won't work?" he inquired with consummate innocence.

"The seduction routine. I'm going to get you out of this house, Alex Steele. I just haven't figured out how to do it yet."

He raised his glass in a toast. "To your enterprise then, darling. I'm going to enjoy watching the wheels turn in that beautiful head of yours."

His rugged features creased into a devastatingly attractive smile and Eve, in self-defense, turned her attention to the table. Mrs. Jacobs had obviously gone all out for his return. The antique Irish linen tablecloth had been spread and set with the best crystal and china. She noted with silent despair that the cut flowers of this afternoon had been replaced with a silver vase filled to overflowing with black-eyed Susans.

Eve risked a questioning glance at her husband. "Mrs. Jacobs did everything else," he murmured, nodding his dark head with a single, brief motion, acknowledging that the perky flowers were his contribution to the dinner. Damn him, she thought, he definitely wasn't going to fight fair!

As other couples might have their restaurant or their song, she and Alex had their flower. And, as incongruous as it might seem to their life-style, that flower was the simple, velvet-faced black-eyed Susan.

They had left the party at her father's palatial estate in Beverly Hills that night, Eve leaving her own car behind as she let Alex lead her to his black Lotus parked in the curving drive. The throaty purr of the car as it wove its way down Sunset Boulevard was the only sound in the close interior of the sleek vehicle.

Eve had the strange feeling she was being kidnapped—

shanghaied by a dark and menacing pirate. She'd never had a man sweep her so instantly off her feet and, at her age, she felt she should know better. But the light, possessive touch of Alex's fingertips as his hand rested on her knee felt like a surging brand, as if the man had staked his claim and would brook no argument on the issue.

She lightly caressed his dark hand, her fingers circling with a slow, delicate touch. His touch tightened on her skin, causing, she knew, a bruise. But there was also a surging warmth that made Eve curious enough to test this phenomenon a bit further.

She ran her fingers up the inside of his arm, rewarded by the hand as it stroked her leg, moving above her knee in perfect rhythm with her own hand's tracing trail up his arm. *Interesting*. She glanced up at the impassive profile that was directed to the curving, twisting roadway.

Eve shifted in the soft leather seat, leaning toward the silent man as her fingers moved to feather lightly over the stern line of his wide shoulders. She could feel his muscles tensing under her sensitive touch, but the only other sign that he noticed was his hand, which moved to slip under the soft chiffon of her dress. A spark ran along the inside of her nylon-clad thigh, but still his attention appeared to be on the roadway.

She grew more intrepid, her fingernails tracing a path up his corded neck. The long fingers on her thigh dug into her skin, making Eve gasp as she felt the strangely pleasurable pain. She risked a glance upward at the man's face. Still no sign of involvement in this experimentation she was carrying out.

Eve returned her hand to her lap, only to have it covered by Alex's strong, dark hand after he let go of her thigh and pulled the chiffon back over her knees. As the road continued winding through the Santa Monica Mountains, curving through Brentwood, on the way to her home in Pacific Palisades, her curiosity got the better of her once again. As long as she sat perfectly still, his roving hand seemed content just to hold hers, his thumb tracing delicate little patterns on her palm.

Eve lifted her fingers, tracing the shell of his ear, feeling the seductive stroking begin once again, this time across the sea-green chiffon covering her stomach. It was as if little tongues of flame were searing the material to her skin, and her head swam with the heat scorching her veins. Her lips tentatively traced a line from his earlobe down the strong, rather forbidding jawline, promptly rewarded as his rogue hand moved across her rib cage.

She was finding it a heady experience, this ability to be the one completely in control. Eve knew that, were she to return her hands to her lap and remove her tingling lips from his warm, fragrant skin, the silent man beside her would cease his erotic caresses. But she didn't want that. Not quite yet. Not until she discovered the full extent of these new-found powers.

She became absolutely lion-hearted, nibbling at his earlobe, catching small bits of flesh between her teeth.

"You know," his voice rumbled like the distant crash of waves on a rocky shore, "if you keep this up, you won't be taken straight home."

She'd finally made him speak! To acknowledge that this surging warmth was not hers alone, that she was capable of causing a degree of havoc to his own senses. But what degree? she wondered. His eyes still hadn't left the road. *What type of man was this?* Eve pressed on further in her quest to find out.

She untied the black bow tie, daring to press her lips against his dark throat. By this time, Eve was far more interested in getting his hand to respond to her wishes than divining the reasons for her highly uncharacteristic behavior.

Eve wondered just how he could drive like this, but the answer came a moment later as he turned the car abruptly off the road and cut the engine.

Still without saying a word, Alex pulled her onto his lap; his strong fingers undid the zipper of her strapless dress and dispensed with the hooks to her bra in a single, deft stroke. Pushing down the material, he lowered his raven head to capture the thrusting crowns of her breasts, while his hand returned to the warmth at the juncture of her thighs under the layers of soft chiffon. Eve twisted against the dual sensations, not knowing which one was driving her more insane. Then, without warning, he zipped up her dress, not bothering to replace the bra, and opened the car door. Turning in his bucket seat, he helped Eve out of the low-slung car and followed right behind her.

"What are you doing?" She watched as he pulled a blanket from behind the seat.

"First lesson, Eve. I only issue a warning once."

His hand about her waist, he led her down a small, winding footpath that carved its way through the Santa Monica Mountains. After they'd lost sight of the road, he spread the blanket out, sinking down onto the ground and pulling her gently with him. The full moon bathed the area in a sparkling iridescence, the shadowed leaness of his high-boned cheeks making him appear almost satanic as he slid the green chiffon down her body.

Alex knelt to take off her high-heeled sandals, feathering her instep and ankles with light, intoxicating little kisses. His fingers ran up her legs, slipping into the waistband of her pantyhose before peeling them off, his lips greeting each bit of newly exposed skin.

Like a character in a surrealistic film, Eve felt as though

some part of her had flown from her body and was operating on a higher, more ethereal plane. She began to undress him in turn, in the moon-spangled darkness, slipping off his shirt, her mouth tasting once again of the warm flavor of his skin. His shoes and socks were no problem, but when her fingers reached the waistband of his slacks, she hesitated, realizing that she was no longer the one in control. Her body's clamoring demands had taken charge and she was struck by the sudden awareness that in her bold and atypical experimentation, she'd spawned a physical hunger that refused to be suppressed. It was an erotic shock to her deepest senses, frightening her with its enormity.

When his dark eyes met her gaze, Eve felt Alex could see all the way to her soul.

"Don't be afraid." His black velvet voice stroked her frayed nerves as he moved to take care of the matter of the dress slacks himself. He left on the low-rise briefs, but with the dark color against his equally dark skin, he might as well have been wearing nothing at all. The scant material hid nothing.

"Your turn," he instructed softly, with just a hint of gentle amusement.

Eve tried to keep her hands from trembling as they reached for the elasticized waistband. The image of a Band-Aid suddenly popped unbidden into her mind. There was always that question of whether you coax it off slowly, so as to minimize the pain, or whip it off, braving sharper pain, but for a shorter time. It seemed the problem with these silky briefs was identical. Should she just gradually lower them, attempting to appear far more relaxed and self-assured than she was about such matters? Or should she close her eyes and give them one fast yank? Eve was not completely inexperienced, but she'd never undressed a man before. Who'd ever suspect it would all come down to a method of Band-Aid removal? The irreverent thought caused a laugh to escape her lips.

Alex propped himself up on his elbows, his black eyes glittering dangerously. "That's a first. I don't think I've ever been laughed at—at quite this point."

Eve shook her honey-blonde hair, scattering pins that would be forever lost in the mountainous Will Rogers State Park, as she laughed harder.

"I'm not laughing at you," she gasped, her nervousness making itself known in this unseemly manner. "I was just thinking about Band-Aids."

"Now that *is* bloody complimentary."

She spluttered with laughter again at his offended tone, knowing by the savage gleam in his eyes that she was getting in deeper with each word.

"No," she struggled to explain, stifling the giggles. The effort resulted in a slightly breathless, silvery tone. "You don't understand."

"Try me."

Eve's hazel eyes coaxed him to give her a chance as she met his baffled expression. "I was trying to decide whether to give a quick tug, or go slowly. I've never done this before," she admitted on a note of apology.

She could feel his tense body relaxing as he gave her a lazy, roguish grin before settling back down onto the blanket.

"Slowly," he instructed. "I like the feel of your hands."

With that problem out of the way, Eve was to discover the consequences of her reckless research. His practiced male hands roamed her body at will, alerting every nerve ending and firing rockets in her whirling mind. His lips followed the blazing path his hands forged, tasting her essence from every burning pore. As Alex brought her to a height of ecstasy she'd never before imagined, Eve clung to him, pressing herself against his hard length until their bodies fused into one white-hot passionate flame. When the shattering release tore through her it seemed to disintegrate her bones and his name rang from her throat, echoing out into the vast night.

She lay with him, legs still entwined on the soft blanket, bathed in languorous contentment, her fingers curling idly in the dark, thick hair under her cheek. For the first time, Eve looked around, seeing that he'd thrown the blanket down into a field of black-eyed Susans. The big white moon lit the wildflowers as they surrounded the pair of lovers, their showy heads bobbing and dancing with apparent approval in the soft night breeze.

Eve shook the distant memory from her mind. "You don't fight fair," she repeated her earlier thoughts aloud.

Alex was not unaffected by the erotic memory he had seen reflected on her face and his voice was unnaturally husky, revealing more of his Irish heritage than usual. "You know the old saying, darling. All's fair in love and war."

"And which is this?"

His dark eyes moved over her, appearing suddenly like windows painted black, revealing nothing of what was going on inside.

"That's up to you, Eve."

They ate the superb dinner Mrs. Jacobs had prepared in a thick, ponderous silence. That is, Alex ate, pushing his empty plate back with a deep groan of satisfaction. He had obviously missed home cooking, Eve noticed, wishing that she could believe he'd missed anything else about his home—such as his wife. He rested his elbows on the table, linking his fingers together as he surveyed her.

"I think you've developed such a taste for creamed chicken on the banquet circuit that it's all you can eat."

Her eyes had been glued to her plate as her mind fought with possible answers to her dilemma. Now they rose reluctantly to the laughter she knew would be waiting for her in his dark caramel gaze.

"What are you talking about, Alex?"

He nodded toward the untouched food on her plate. "You haven't eaten a thing. Shall I have Mrs. Jacobs try to rustle up some rubber chicken and canned gravy for you?"

Eve shook her head. "No, thank you."

"Hey, it wasn't a very good one, but it *was* supposed to be a joke. Don't I get even a little smile?"

The grin under his dark mustache was beguiling, enticing, just like a fisherman who's cast out a very bright lure. She could almost feel the tugging on her inner self as he began to slowly reel the line back in, drawing her into complacency.

"This entire situation isn't funny, Alex." Eve pressed her lips into a hard line.

"It was funny in *Philadelphia Story*. Why don't you try thinking of me as Cary Grant? And yourself as Katharine Hepburn?" he suggested, grinning wider.

"In the first place, you're no Cary Grant. And life is not a movie, Alex Steele. You don't get your unchallenged director's control around my house."

"You're not Kate Hepburn either, sweetheart," he murmured. "But, we've always been able to strike a few sparks off each other."

"Please—"

Alex heaved a frustrated sigh. "All right. But what do

you suggest we do with that perfectly browned game hen? We don't own a dog.'' He arched a jet brow. ''Or has that changed, too?''

''No. No dog. No dogs, cats, hamsters—not even a parakeet.'' No pets. But then pets were for children, weren't they? And there'd never be any children running through the rooms of this house.

''Maybe we need one,'' he mused. ''Do you think we'd be a more typical American family if we got a dog? What type would you fancy, darling? St. Bernard, perhaps? Nice for skiing trips. We could fill the cask with imported peach brandy.''

Alex rubbed his craggy, thrusting jaw thoughtfully as Eve shook her head in a strong negative gesture. ''How about a German shepherd? We had one of those in *The Seraglio Syndrome*. He was easy to work with . . . Cocker spaniel? One with the golden, pulled-taffy color of your hair?''

If he heard her softly issued protest, Alex chose to ignore it, continuing to ponder the subject of dog ownership. ''We should probably consider your image. What type of dogs do the voters go for these days?''

''Stop it!'' Eve jumped up from the table, her eyes moist as she looked down into his teasing face.

''Stop what?'' He took a sip of dark, fragrant coffee, eyeing her thoughtfully over the rim of the cup.

Eve tried to control the tremor in her voice, but it was there. Thin and ragged. ''Please stop tormenting me.''

Damn. If there was one thing he'd never wanted to do, it was make Eve cry. Yet they seemed unable to avoid hurting each other. What she had done after Mexico had torn his heart to ribbons. It was only after he realized how deeply he loved her that he'd determined to put the past behind them.

There was a shadowing in his deep brown eyes at her accusing stance. His saddened gaze took in her fingers as they clutched the edge of the table, gathering the linen into ruffled lines, her knuckles stark white with nervous pressure.

Alex shook his head with silent despair. "Sit down, Eve, and relax. I didn't mean to torment you. I was just trying to lighten up the gloomy atmosphere in here. I've got this feeling Scotty should be playing 'Amazing Grace' on his bagpipes while we eulogize the brave and noble Mr. Spock."

Eve sank wearily into her chair, resting her forehead on her fingertips. "That's all everything is to you, isn't it, Alex? A scene from some movie. *Philadelphia Story*. *Star Trek*. Just one series of flickering Technicolor images after another."

"Is that what you think?" Alex looked honestly interested in her opinion.

"Doesn't it fit?"

A slow smile lifted the corners of the harsh lips. A smile that, she realized, was momentarily directed inward.

"At times," he admitted. "We all have our methods, Eve. You slip into that cool sophistication each morning with your clothing, that mask of glacial competence you wear so well. Sometimes, it even helps you feel a bit like the person you're pretending to be, doesn't it?"

He seemed satisfied with the flush of color that darkened her cheeks at his blunt appraisal and continued. "But inside that classic bone structure and Grace Kelly–Meryl Streep exterior, there's a warm, passionate woman. A vulnerable woman who's capable of a dizzying range of emotions. Feelings you've learned to hide extraordinarily well. Self-protective coloring, sweetheart."

"And you?"

"And I fall behind my mask of witty urbanity and droll professionalism. I tend to talk in terms of what I do best. What I do very well, if I may be so immodest as to add. It bolsters my confidence, as well as reminding my adversary that I'm a force to be reckoned with."

Alex could have added that it helped him remember how far he'd come. That this house, and the life-style that came with it, were a long way from that war-torn tenement he'd grown up in. But he had never told Eve about those days and he wasn't about to now. She'd only accuse him of playing to her sympathies. He wanted a lot from his wife—her love, her life—but never her pity.

"Then I'm your adversary?" That was, Eve knew, a dangerous position to be in.

The edge of his mouth hardened. "You seem to have shot the opening volley."

Eve's eyes widened. "Me? It was *you* who planted that damn story! You admitted it."

"Of course. But only in retaliation for that ridiculous set of divorce papers you had served on me. Christ, Eve," he agonized, his voice harsh, "you could at least have called and warned me those bloody things were coming."

"I didn't think you'd care."

"*Care?* Do you want to know just how much I cared?" A muscle jumped in his jaw. "Do you have any idea how much it cost for me to get drunk for three whole days? Would you care to know how many members of the crew sat around drawing union pay while I tried to drown Eve Meredith Steele in several bottles of horribly inferior scotch?"

She couldn't answer as she fought back the threatening tears. He'd begun the damn thing in Mexico. Why was she feeling sorry for him? Why should she care if the man drank himself into doomsday?

"Eve?"

She shook her head wordlessly, dark lashes resting against her cheeks as she dropped her eyes back to her plate.

"I'd like to suggest a cease-fire," Alex said softly.

"I don't—"

He raised a hand to quell her protest. "All right. Then let's at least set some rules of war. Something akin to the Geneva Convention. We'll call it the Pacific Palisades Plan, okay?"

"Cute title. Try making it into a two-hour spy thriller and you might just have something, Alex."

"Is there another man?"

The question came from left field, and her shocked eyes flew to his face, giving him the answer he needed.

"No. I didn't think so. Look, Eve, I've spent the past months giving our relationship a lot of thought. I don't want you out of my life. Ever. I know you're convinced everything's over between us, but what will it hurt if I live here while you finish out the campaign? It certainly wouldn't harm your reelection chances. Then, if you still want the divorce—if I haven't convinced you that you need me every bit as much as I need you—I'll pack up and move out without another word."

"Just like that?"

"Just like that. But I'm warning you, Eve, I'm known for a stubborn streak a mile wide. And I'm incredibly selfish. I don't intend to lose you."

Eve felt braver after his calmly stated proposition. There seemed to be no problem, after all. She certainly wouldn't change her mind. She'd had plenty of lonely nights to consider the folly of her marriage to this man. The campaign only had another few weeks. Then, win or lose, she could get on with her life.

"Let me see if I've got this straight." She studied him with a measurable amount of suspicion. "I agree to let you stay here for the few weeks remaining in the campaign and in return I can have my divorce?"

"You'll have it," he confirmed. "Quick and easy and not another word from me." Alex thrust a dark hand across the table. "Deal?"

Eve took his hand, feeling a little like Snow White when offered the poison apple by the Wicked Stepmother. "Deal."

"Then it's settled." Alex sat back with an obvious air of satisfaction. "But rest assured, darling, you're not going to want that divorce."

"You promised, Alex!"

"So I did. And I'll do nothing to compromise your honor or your campaign. I do, however, intend to wage a winning campaign of my own on this domestic battlefield, Eve. I've figured out what went wrong the first time and I'm here to set matters straight."

I know damn well what went wrong, Eve thought to herself. But she was interested in his diagnosis.

"All right. You're going to tell me anyway. So, what went wrong?"

"I moved too fast. I walked into a party where I was expecting to be bored to tears and spied the most beautiful, most womanly vision I'd ever encountered. Bang! Just like that, I had to have you. And, never having been known for my patience, I swept you off and married you before you had a chance to entertain second thoughts. I was scheduled to do that damn film in Mexico and wanted you to be my wife before I left. Which only gave us three months to get to know one another.

"Three lousy months, and you ended up spending half that time in Sacramento. Hell, the Governor saw more of you than I did. I doubt if we had more than three words of meaningful dialogue that entire time because whenever you made it home, we'd try to brush away our problems upstairs in bed. I was jealous of your career, Eve, I'll admit to that now."

"Jealous?"

He nodded, his lips set in a firm, taut line. "Jealous of the time it took you away from me. But instead of talking it out, I just let the resentment build up until it exploded in Mexico. Consequently, you never did discover just how charming I can be. A slight omission I intend to begin working on immediately."

Eve eyed him warily, knowing this was probably the moment to run from the room and double-bolt the guest room door. "What, exactly, do you mean by that?"

"What I mean, Eve, is that I plan to court you in style this time. I plan on filling that little china cup of your life with Alex Steele until it's overflowing, love."

She folded her arms across her chest. "You're aiming at a target who's moved out of range, Alex. I'm warning you, my mind is made up. My feet are set in concrete, or whatever other little clichés you might think up to fit this situation."

He gave her a thoroughly devastating grin. "Ah, but you're underestimating me. You haven't had the opportunity to see your husband decked out in full battle regalia."

"John Wayne?" Eve smiled in spite of herself at his almost youthful enthusiasm for the quest.

The boisterous answering grin extended to his eyes, the dark color sparked with shared humor. "Too dated, darling. Harrison Ford or Tom Selleck at least."

"At least," she murmured, beginning to relax slightly. A fatal miscalculation, she was to realize momentarily.

It's always a mistake to drop your guard when the enemy's on the march.

"One thing you can be certain of, Eve. There'll be no unexpected pregnancies this time."

All the color fled from her face and Eve felt as if a cold, clammy fist had just clenched her heart. Even now, after these months of healing, the memory could bring such sweeping waves of pain, Eve thought she'd be ill. She rose unsteadily to her feet, knocking over her wine glass. The red liquid left a spreading stain on the tablecloth. Like blood. Alex Steele had just won this skirmish; it was time to retreat. She fled the battleground.

Damn. Now what?

"Eve?" he called after her, concern evident in his tone as he followed her from the room.

Alex paused in the guest room doorway, his dark gaze settling on the woman slumped miserably on the edge of the bed.

"Eve?" His questioning tone was hesitant, lacking the usual ring of cocky self-assurance. She had put up a wall between them and he didn't know how to breach it.

Her only response was a slow shake of her head. She couldn't look at him. Wouldn't look at him. She'd known Alex could be a ruthless adversary, she'd heard the stories about people who had thought they could stand in his way. They'd been mowed down without having time to realize the error of their ways. Business adversaries and women, his reputation with both had always been brutal.

What had ever made her think she would be dealt with differently? Alex Steele was a self-made man. Whatever he'd done to achieve the power he now held, he'd done it on his own. Eve knew enough about Alex to know the man was ruthless, but bringing up their poor dead baby was a treacherous blow she hadn't expected even from him.

He was standing over her now, but still Eve refused to look up. With every bit of strength she possessed, she tried to concentrate on the soft, swirling pattern of the rose Aubusson carpet under her feet. When that didn't work, she tried reciting the multiplication tables in her head, all the way through the twelves. Alex hadn't said anything more, but Eve knew he was still there. She could feel his unwavering gaze.

She moved on to conjugating irregular Spanish verbs, her mind reaching for the tenses like a lifeline. She clutched tightly to the comforter on either side of her taut body, willing herself not to look up at him. But, like a child's marionette, controlled by some devilish imp rebelliously pulling the strings, Eve turned, looking up at his thick waves of hair. They were disturbed, as if he'd been forcing his fingers through them in angry frustration. The dark eyes pierced her from under heavy black brows.

"We're going to discuss it, Eve. Because unless we do, we don't stand a chance."

He had the grace to wince, Eve noted, as she stared at him, her face twisted with a bitterness that was at odds with the almost perfect symmetry of her features.

"I tried to tell you downstairs, Alex. We had our chance. *You* had your chance. All I want is to be left in peace for the remainder of this charade. And that includes *never* discussing our baby with you."

The tone she'd discovered lurking somewhere deep inside her was cool and collected, amazing her as she didn't even choke on the words. Perhaps she should have been an actress, she thought for one wild, fleeting moment.

"Wrong, sweetheart," Alex returned, his voice a low, silky warning. "You agreed to my terms and they never included leaving you in peace. On the contrary, Eve, I was quite specific about my intent. I plan to woo you, win you and make wild, passionate love to you. The sequence of events is entirely up to you. But all three things will most definitely take place. And we *will* discuss Mexico and everything that happened there. As well as the resulting fallout from your little bombshell."

Eve checked herself with visible restraint, stopping the hysterical words that had been about to fly off her tongue. Instead, she turned her wrist slightly to glance down at her watch, giving what she hoped was a believable performance.

"Alex," she appealed softly, "you must be exhausted. It's morning in London, it's late in Peoria, and it's even late in Los Angeles. Barry has a tough schedule lined up for me tomorrow. Could we continue this conversation some other time?"

She stifled a false yawn, slightly surprised when the act triggered an actual one. She was tired, she realized, exhausted from the emotional events of the day.

His harsh face softened. "Okay, Eve. We'll call an eight-hour cease-fire. But, I'm warning you—tomorrow I come out shooting the moment I see the whites of your lovely hazel eyes."

Don't you dare respond to that crooning, seductive tone, Eve commanded her softening heart. This is war, remember? We're talking life or death here.

"If you don't let me get to sleep, those whites will be terribly red, Alex."

He bent quickly, planting a peck on her lips, the sudden heat disintegrating as he pulled back.

"Good night, love." His dark eyes gleamed with a swift, hungry light. "I don't suppose there's a chance you've taken to walking in your sleep?"

Like down the hallway? Good try. And surely the shortest cease-fire on record, Eve thought.

"No. I haven't."

"Too bad," he murmured, thrusting his hands into his pockets and sauntering from the room.

Eve rose from the bed, taking her clothes off and hanging them in the closet. She was suddenly sapped of all vestiges of strength. She quickly brushed her teeth, made only a half-hearted effort at washing her face, and skipped the nightly ritual of hair-brushing entirely. She set the clock radio for five-thirty, thinking she didn't need an alarm because she wouldn't be getting any sleep.

With Alex Steele in residence just two doors down the hall, she'd be awake all night. She rolled over onto her stomach, clutching her pillow as she buried her head into the soft down, and fell instantly into a deep, dreamless sleep.

# Chapter Four

"Why are morning deejays so disgustingly cheerful?"

Eve reached over to hit the switch on the radio, silencing the enthusiastic gibberish filtering into her ear. "I suppose misery loves company. If they have to be up at this ungodly hour, everyone else should be, too."

She blinked her eyes in the pearly dawn light; the unfamiliar surroundings at first startled her. Then, her sleep-hazed mind began to recollect the events of the previous day.

"Alex," she moaned, wishing she could just stay in bed and pull the covers over her head until the election and his personal campaign were over.

Instead she slipped into a sunshine-yellow tee shirt and white shorts and stealthily crept through the bedroom doorway. She tiptoed down the hallway, relieved when she discovered the door to the master bedroom closed. Taking into consideration that even the great Alex Steele must be susceptible to jet-lag, Eve decided she'd probably be well into her morning schedule before he awoke. With any luck, she wouldn't see the man all day.

She made her way down the long, curving stairway, only breathing easily when she reached the steps outside the double front door. Then she turned, palms pressed against the heavily carved wood as she pushed herself into it, stretching the muscles at the back of her calves. Eve could feel her blood beginning to circulate in a comforting glow as she stretched and warmed up her slender body.

Then, tossing back her dark blonde hair, which she'd tied with an elastic band, Eve began to run down the sidewalk, through the quiet, peaceful neighborhood. There were a few other runners out today, the same members of the physical fitness fraternity she saw every day at this time. Strangers who were not quite that, since they shared the pink dawn together each morning.

Every so often she glanced down to check her wide-strapped watch, knowing exactly where she wanted to be at each familiar checkpoint. When she'd gone nearly five miles, she broke into a dead run, sprinting the remainder of the way home, her lungs straining, her face alive with the glow of physical exertion.

Eve was panting in deep but comfortable gulps when she reached out for the heavy door handle, almost tumbling into the foyer as the door opened in front of her.

"Alex!" It was a gasp, not so much because she was surprised to see him, but because she was winded.

His appearance certainly didn't help her catch her absent breath. His dark hair was flattened with moisture and he was clad only in a pair of brief black swim trunks. Eve directed her attention to the safety of the floor, where he was dripping water onto the gleaming parquet.

"Don't you have a towel?"

"Forgot it," he admitted cheerily. "I was a little off in timing you. You've gotten faster."

Eve stretched to the side, both arms above her head as she leaned slowly in each direction, allowing her muscles to cool down slowly so she wouldn't cramp. Her breathing was still a bit weak and she bent forward, hands on her knees as she drank in a few deep, clearing breaths.

As she stood back up, Eve noticed Alex studying her body with a measured, practiced scrutiny. She felt at a distinct disadvantage, with her hair clinging to her forehead in damp curls and the glistening of perspiration on her upper lip. She watched his gaze settle momentarily on the damp shadow darkening the tee shirt between her breasts before moving down her gleaming, moist legs.

"Yep. Faster," he repeated finally. "I'd planned to meet you at the door with this, but you almost beat me to it." He pulled a tall glass from behind his back. "Good morning." He offered it to her.

Eve took a tentative sip and looked up at him in surprise. "This is fresh-squeezed. Mrs. Jacobs never makes fresh orange juice."

"I made it."

"You?" She couldn't remember ever seeing this man in the kitchen.

"Yes, me. And didn't those nuns ever teach you that it's a mortal sin to live in California and drink the frozen stuff? I've spent the last six months bragging to all those British film folk about the wonders of living in Lotus Land, and fresh orange juice was definitely one of the perks. That and beautiful women, of course." His warm gaze skimmed down her body, returning to her face, the fine network of lines crinkling at the corners of his dark eyes.

Eve admitted, to her most secret self, that this juice was probably the best she'd ever tasted. Coming at right this moment, when she was hot and sweaty, she knew the finest Dom Perignon couldn't come close. It was uncharacteristically sweet of him. And sweet was one description she had never heard applied to Alex Steele. She knew she should thank him; she could tell by the expectant gleam in his eyes that he was waiting.

"I see you've been swimming," she said instead, her eyes moving pointedly to the puddles on the dark squares of hardwood.

"Another California perk I've missed. I thought about running this morning, but I didn't know if you'd want my company just yet, so I opted for a few quick laps."

The truth of the matter was that he'd had to force himself to stay in the bedroom when he heard her stealthy footsteps earlier. He'd been wide awake, after a night of foolishly hoping she'd succumb to old memories and join him in that wide, incredibly lonely bed.

"You should have joined me, I would have loved your company," Eve replied, her hazel eyes wide and innocent.

"Really?"

She almost, just barely, hated herself for baiting him when she saw his undisguised look of pleasure. He appeared surprisingly boyish, and almost vulnerable. But looks could be deceiving, Eve reminded herself, getting a grip on her strangely tumbling heart.

"Of course," she taunted sweetly, "I would have run much, much faster with you in pursuit, Alex. Probably could have broken my time . . . Thanks for the juice." She handed him the empty glass and ran up the stairs to her room, hearing the delayed burst of deep laughter when she was halfway there.

"What are you doing?" Eve eyed the man lounging on the living room sofa.

"Reading." Alex held up the *Newsweek* for her perusal.

"I can see that and it's not what I meant. What are you doing all dressed up like that?" Her eyes took in his hand-tailored navy suit, white silk shirt and slim, wine-red tie. She could see a gleam of gold at his turned-back cuffs.

"Don't I pass inspection? This is all a little new to me. I read an article coming over on the Concorde, detailing the wardrobe for a candidate's spouse, but it wasn't a lot of help. I don't have a basic black dress, slim pocketbook or pumps. But I did my best."

Eve steadied herself with an effort. "Do you mean to tell me you're coming along today? Is that what all this"—she waved her hand at his impeccable appearance—"is about?"

His brown eyes danced with merriment. "Of course."

She expelled her breath through tightly compressed lips. "That's why you weren't upset at Barry's little innuendo yesterday, about the two of us spending an intimate day together."

Alex flipped the magazine onto the glass-topped table in front of him. "Of course I wasn't upset. You're still my wife and I trust you. But I'm glad to see you could recognize his little game for what it was. He doesn't worry me."

"I think you're underestimating the man," Eve retorted. "Barry happens to be a consummate political strategist. He's not just another pretty face, you know, Alex." She crossed her arms in front of herself and scowled into his laughing face.

"I know that. I've heard all about him. He's reported to be terrific at his job. A real shark." Alex grinned at her with a provocative leer. "But I know for a fact that you like your male animals a lot more warm-blooded."

The light of battle stormed in her eyes as Eve opened her mouth to destroy the man with a few well-chosen words. But the doorbell rang, forestalling her furious argument.

"All set?" Barry walked past her with the air of one who had spent a great deal of time in the house and felt immensely comfortable. He skidded to an abrupt halt when he spotted Alex.

"What's *he* doing?" he asked Eve, jerking his thumb in the direction of her husband.

"He's coming with us." Her tone held a note of self-assurance that came from regularly having others defer to her wishes. Everyone except Alex Steele, she thought, sensing his satisfaction as he watched her distraught associate.

"You didn't say anything about this yesterday." Barry's gray eyes flashed coldly.

Eve could have killed Alex without a single shred of mercy, she considered blackly as he ambled over to slip his hand possessively about her waist. His white teeth flashed in his dark face with a broad, insinuating curl.

"Last night," his deep voice was confident, "my wife and I had our little reunion and came to several agreements. But the only one that might possibly concern you, Matthews, as Eve's aide, is that you can count on my company at all of her future campaign appearances."

"Eve?"

Why was Barry always seeking confirmation of Alex's words and behavior from her? Eve wondered with a spark of irritation. What in the world made the man think she or anyone else had a smidgen of control over what Alex Steele did?

"We'd better get going," she dodged the loaded question blandly, casting a glance at her gold watch. "We just have enough time to make that Rotary breakfast, Barry."

His mouth drew into a hard line as he jerked his head in a swift, accepting nod. There was a slight traffic jam in the doorway as Alex and Barry both manuevered for position and Eve sighed wearily. This was going to be a very long day.

If Eve was at first nervous with Alex seated to her left during the breakfast meeting, his easygoing attitude eventually allowed her to relax. By the time the plates had been cleared away, she felt prepared to give her short speech before opening the floor to questions. Each special-interest group always had its own area of concern and on a day like today, she might have to address several issues in depth.

She knew she was fortunate to have Barry as an aide. He always filled her in as they made their way to various speaking engagements, providing her with a vast storehouse of information, facts and figures he expected her to need at each upcoming stop. Her possession of an almost photographic memory didn't hurt, either.

She had expected to receive a number of questions about her endorsement of investment pooling for state funds, this group being heavily business-oriented, but instead, the focus of attention seemed to be directed at Alex and their relationship. Eve felt the beginning twinges of a headache, wondering why she was even surprised by the interest in her personal life.

She and Alex had lived in glass houses long before their marriage. Her political career and family ties to Olympus Studios kept her in the public spotlight. While Alex had a compelling background and had built himself a fantastic career, she had a feeling he would have drawn attention to himself whatever he'd done. Put them together and there was seldom a day that went by when Eve didn't pass a rack in the supermarket and see some new, ridiculous gossip about herself.

"Senator Steele!" A hand shot up and Eve recognized a

banker who'd openly supported her opponent in the primary election. Knowing she was in for it, she smiled as she opened Pandora's box.

"Yes?"

"You've been quoted as saying that your bonding proposal will bail out the flagging film industry. But aren't you really catering to a special-interest group whose members are more familiar with caviar than hamburger? At a time when everyone's tightening belts, how can you justify expenditures for escapist entertainment?"

Eve smiled graciously before beginning a defense of her position. "I'm afraid the commonly held image that the motion picture industry revolves around a handful of visible moguls is inaccurate. There are over thirty thousand people in this valley who are directly dependent on the industry for their paychecks. And, of course, you have all the shopkeepers and service workers who derive employment from them. It's very important to Los Angeles, and the state, that something be done to breathe new life into the business. I consider bond sales to finance California projects a sound, practical answer."

The balding, forceful man stuck to the subject with all the tenacity of ants at a Fourth of July picnic. "If California depends so heavily on American-made movies, how can you explain the fact that your very own foreign-born husband has completed two films in the last year which were both shot on location out of the country? Where will he be taking California dollars next?"

Eve's hands were clasped behind her back and she felt a tight, reassuring squeeze as Alex rose beside her, effectively drawing all attention to himself.

"I'll readily admit to being the black sheep of the family," he said with disarming candor, his smile inviting answering ones from the audience. "I would like to remind everyone that, by virtue of an American mother, I am a U.S. citizen. In fact, I'm looking forward to casting my first vote in America for my wife." He gave Eve a warm, encouraging look before continuing to answer the baited question.

"I'm hoping California voters are intelligent enough not to blame a candidate for the fact that it was impossible for her husband to find a location in the U.S. to film a believable remake of *Wuthering Heights*." Alex held up his right hand in the gesture of a pledge and smiled. "Believe me, gentlemen, the next project I take on will be a Western."

There was a ripple of comfortable laughter and Eve was relieved when the questioning changed to investment pooling.

"I enjoyed that."

Eve turned to the man seated by her side in the back seat of the comfortable Chrysler. "Really," she teased, with a light smile, "I'd have thought eggs Benedict more to your liking than runny scrambled eggs."

"Wasn't that what I was eating?" Alex's dark eyebrows soared upward in mock surprise. "I guess I was so taken with the company I failed to notice."

"Flattery," Eve murmured, leafing through some papers on her lap, "will get you nowhere."

"Then I'll just have to resort to more tried and true methods." His smooth voice was laced with a laconic Irish brogue and laughter spiked Alex's eyes as he lightly grasped the back of her neck. His dark head swooped down to capture her lips in an intense, short kiss.

A spark ran up the delicate bones of her spine as Eve felt his mustache lightly tickle her skin, the mobile lips below it molding her mouth. It was only a brief encounter, but it shook her to her toes.

"Alex," she hissed, glancing guiltily toward the front of the car, where she caught Barry's cold silver eyes in the rearview mirror, "stop that!"

He covered her hand with his, linking their fingers together as he brought her wrist to his smiling lips, gracing her sensitive skin with soft kisses.

"You said you were impervious to flattery," he reminded her. "A good general never takes to the field without an alternate battle strategy." His cheek creased as he gave her a slow, triumphant smile.

Eve fought the surge of color that flowed into her cheeks as she turned her attention back to the papers on her lap. They might as well have been written in Sanskrit, for all the good it did her. She was too intensely aware of the man next to her, her lips feeling somehow deprived of the warm pleasure he'd brought to the kiss.

It was a long day, and wearying. Among the scheduled appearances were two at senior citizens' centers. As a rule, the senior audiences were usually among those most interested in the issues, only a few opting for a game of chess or checkers instead of an opportunity to question the candidate. Eve noted with a trace of benign amusement that today Alex seemed to be getting the lion's share of attention. She'd seen more than one blue-haired lady fussing with her curls at his arrival.

The man definitely had something, she mused, allowing her thoughts to drift momentarily as she watched him charm a clutch of elderly women. Charisma, that aura of sexual magnetism—whatever it was, it seemed to span the generations. Females of every age were drawn to Alex Steele, like fire follows a flammable vapor. Almost as if her thoughts had communicated themselves to him, Alex turned toward her, giving her a warm, conspiratorial wink. Eve shook her head slightly, smiling with reluctant admiration across the room.

They didn't stop for lunch, opting instead for the traditional foods offered in the various neighborhoods they visited. Eve had become an expert at this, balancing her stuffed grape leaves on a paper plate with one hand as she deftly shook hands with the other at a Greek fair. Another stop, this time in a barrio community to discuss the plight of undocumented workers, brought a similar plate, holding a tamale.

They'd picked up a contingent of press along the way and Alex smiled a slight apology as the questions continued to prove more often personal than political. Everyone finally seemed satisfied when he accepted a plate of nachos and held out a melted-cheese-covered chip, feeding it to Eve as shutters snapped around them. She was beginning to hate the hyped media event, but her politican's mask was firmly in place and she smiled sweetly at her grinning husband.

The evening hours brought a dinner at a meeting of Asian business leaders where Eve was asked a question by a young Chinese engineer, at the precise moment when she'd bitten into a serving of *la chico ch'ao chi*, chicken stuffed with peppers. Of Szechwanese origin, the dish had the effect of instantly clearing her sinuses and making her forget the question all in one brief, peppery second. It took all the control Eve could muster not to flame like a distraught dragon.

It was late when they finally returned home. She sank into a chair, allowing Alex to put the water on for their tea.

"Whew." His fatigue showed in his long, exhaled breath. "This was quite a day. I've never shaken so many hands in my life.'' He rubbed the bottom of his thumb. ''I think I'm getting a blister.''

Eve laughed. ''Don't worry, Alex. After a while you get calluses.''

''Now that's an unattractive prospect,'' he grimaced, setting the teapot on the table.

He poured two steaming cups of the robust English Breakfast tea. Eve shook her head to both sugar and cream. There were far too many opportunities to gain weight on the campaign trail as it was. She'd learned to only sample items, moving things around on her plate with consummate skill. They drank for a time in peaceful companionship, then Alex broke the silence.

''Is it really necessary for you to make all these appearances? It's not like you're a movie star or anything.''

Trust Alex Steele to see his business as more important than hers, Eve thought resignedly.

''I think the people deserve a chance to meet their state senator,'' she stated, running her finger around the rim of the teacup.

''But take that ground-breaking today. Surely that was nothing more than campaign hype,'' he pressed his case.

Eve knew what he was doing. During their brief, stormy relationship, they'd fought continually over her long work hours. If Alex could get her to admit that much of her work was unnecessary, he'd win a major point in their career–marriage conflict.

''It's vital to the interests of the state that we attract new businesses to California, Alex. We try to do that through tax incentives, attractive zoning and good old Chamber of Commerce sales campaigns. A company like Video-Tec will employ a thousand Los Angeles citizens and put a lot of money into our tax coffers. The least I can do is demonstrate my appreciation by showing up for their ground-breaking ceremony."

"I never thought of it that way," he admitted. "I'd always seen those newspaper photos as just another way to get a candidate's face in front of the voters."

Eve pushed her chair back from the table and took her cup and saucer over to the dishwasher. Then, giving him a saucy grin, she confessed, "They're pretty good for that, too."

Despite the smile brightening her face, Alex could see the lines of exhaustion etched on her features. She'd been on display all day—smiling at the proper moments, saying all the right things, accepting questions that bordered on poor taste about her personal life. Matthews had been an almanac of information between stops, but when Eve took center stage, she'd held it alone. Sans props, scripts, supporting actors or retakes. She'd handled the spotlight amazingly well, he realized with a reluctant awe. Alex had never seen his wife operate in the public arena.

"You look tired." He voiced his concern. "Why don't you run up to bed? I'll put the rest of this away."

Eve rubbed her fingertips across her temples. "You don't mind?"

"Not at all. Go to bed, love. I'll see you in the morning." Alex hesitated. "Would you mind company on your run tomorrow?"

Eve felt her heart melt as she heard the uncharacteristic hesitancy in his voice. She couldn't remember hearing Alex ever ask for anything from anyone.

"Not at all, as long as you're able to keep up," she teased lightly. She began to leave the room, then turned to pause in the doorway.

"By the way, Alex, I enjoyed your company today. Thanks for coming."

"Thank you for putting up with a mere political amateur," he answered.

Eve dragged her eyes away from his melted-chocolate gaze and waved her fingers. "Well, good night, then."

"Good night, love."

As she climbed the stairs to the guest room, Eve heard Alex merrily whistling out of tune.

The days continued in much the same manner. Eve and Alex would run in the mornings, gearing up for eighteen hours of frantic activity as they followed Barry's packed itinerary. It was as if her aide and campaign manager had planned for her to personally meet every one of her constituents. By the end of the week, Eve decided they must have put enough miles on the Chrysler to reach to the moon and back.

Sharing a late-night snack in the kitchen was the perfect way to end the day, although after congratulating herself on avoiding sensual snares, Eve began to realize that Alex seemed to have given up on his vow to woo her, win her and make love to her. He'd been friendly, supportive, even amazingly sweet, but he'd made no attempt to reinitiate their lovemaking. If anything, Alex seemed oblivious to the desire that was stretching her nerves to the screeching point.

By the fifth day of their joint campaigning, Eve had seriously considered throwing herself at the man, pinning him to the plush material of the Chrysler's back seat.

That evening ended with a party fund-raising dinner given at the distinctive Westwood Marquis Hotel, located in the fashionable Beverly Hills and Westwood Village area. There were several veiled references to Alex's presence, but Eve experienced relief as he handled the questions like a born diplomat. By the time they arrived home, Eve knew he had successfully alleviated any fears the party might be having about his unexpected reappearance. In fact, she considered wryly, they'd probably drop her from the ticket if she were to kick him out before the election.

"Whew! No one can accuse you of not making the most of your congressional vacation," Alex said, loosening his tie and unbuttoning the first button of his white shirt. He ran his finger around inside the collar. "You put in quite a day, Senator Steele."

Eve collapsed onto the sofa, kicking off her gray pumps and wiggling her toes. "Aah." She breathed in a deep sigh of relief as her feet exulted in their freedom. "I should have been born in the good old days when all this was taken care of in a single, smoke-filled room by a bunch of old party faithfuls and a pocket full of bribe money."

Alex moved behind her, reaching down to massage the muscles at the back of her neck with firm but gentle fingers.

"No," he contradicted her. "Because in those days, my darling, you wouldn't have been allowed in that smoke-filled room. That was not the niche we men had carved out for women in our nice, safe little world."

"God, that feels good." Eve rotated her head in slow circles, loving the feel of his probing fingers as they kneaded the tense muscles of her shoulders. "And just where would I have been in this utopian male state?"

"Barefoot and pregnant at home, of course. Breathlessly awaiting the arrival of your adored husband."

As soon as he said the words, Alex realized he'd blundered into dangerous waters, but he fought for composure, his massaging fingers unceasing in their gentle motions, giving away none of his discomfort.

Eve had to reach deep down inside her for the strength

to continue this conversation without revealing her pain. Alex seemed intent upon insinuating himself firmly back into her life and it was apparent that he intended to weaken all her lines of defense in order to achieve that.

"Barefoot, I'll buy," she agreed with far more aplomb than she felt. "The pregnant—now that would have to be lobbied in great depth."

His hands moved to slip off her rose linen jacket, and his fingers manipulated her clenched muscles under the gray silk blouse.

"Would you care for me to provide you with a position paper on the subject, Senator?" he asked softly. Fools rush in, he tacked on mentally, deciding he was a masochist to even broach the subject of Eve's unwillingness to give up her career for motherhood.

"Only if you're willing to openly declare yourself as a lobbyist," she answered. "But I wouldn't bother if I were you, Alex. According to the doctors at Hillcrest, it's a moot point anyway."

His fingers slipped, digging into her shoulder blades. "What the hell do you mean by that?"

His harsh voice instantly banished the little cloud of self-pity the memory created. Eve looked up, more than a little frightened by his face, which had darkened into a puzzled frown. Deep lines were etched between his eyebrows, and the tightly clenched muscles of his jaw jerked ominously.

The air was suddenly static, and Eve squared her shoulders in a futile attempt to shake off his tense grip.

"It's simple, Alex. You hit the nail right on the head when you said there'd be no unexpected pregnancies for me. That little problem is all taken care of." Her voice was cold and brittle as Eve tried to hide the pain caused by that bizarre twist of fate. She had learned to live with the fact that she'd never have children. It was an unpleasant reality, but her life had known its share of those. Eve had survived by learning at an early age the necessity of depending only on herself, which gave her the ability to land on her own two feet.

"Damn," he grated out between tight lips. "I never thought you'd do anything like that. Don't you need a husband's signature for sterilization? Or are they willing to overlook little niceties like that at private Beverly Hills hospitals?"

Eve was stunned by his gritty, injured tone. The man had colossal nerve, she had to give him that.

"In the first place, you weren't around to sign anything, Alex. In the second place, my sterility was not planned. It was an unfortunate side effect of the infection."

"Infection?" His rugged face was gray. "I should have been there," he muttered, his obsidian eyes staring bleakly at nothing. "I could have stopped it."

"You're right, Alex. You should have been there. But you couldn't have stopped anything. It just happened." As miserable as the memory made her, Eve was growing extremely uncomfortable by his brooding expression. "There's nothing either of us can do about it now."

Alex rubbed his hand over his face; his lips, as they returned into view, were set in a humorless line of resignation. There was an unfamiliar pain in his dark eyes and Eve had to hold her hands together tightly in her lap to keep from pressing her palm against his strangely ashen face. Hadn't he known? Her father said he'd sent Alex the telegram. But even if her inability to become pregnant was a surprise, he'd certainly known about the miscarriage. And she hadn't seen him hurrying to her side then.

So that's how it was, Alex thought miserably. It didn't

alter the fact that he wanted Eve; he hadn't expected her to acquiesce to the notion of a family anyway. But damn, he still felt like hell when he considered how cavalierly she'd rid her body of their child.

"You're right," he agreed hollowly. "And although I was the one insisting we talk about it, I think we're both too tired tonight to be reasonable about the subject. Would you like a nightcap?"

Eve experienced a flood of relief as Alex changed the subject. "That's a good idea," she agreed. "What would you like?"

"I'll get it." He bent down to lightly graze her earlobe with his lips. "You've been working all day."

Eve felt a bittersweet regret as she watched him leave the room. They seemed destined to bring each other grief. Where had everything gone wrong? she wondered bleakly.

Alex had regained control by the time he returned with two glasses of brandy, his smile revealing only a hint of rueful reminiscence. They were sharing the same thoughts once again, she realized. The same regrets.

She took a sip, allowing the warmth to flow through her, unwinding the lingering threads of tension.

"You're really something, you know." His baritone voice was low and admiring as it broke the reflective silence.

Eve turned to look at him as he joined her on the French provincial sofa. His caramel-brown eyes were incredibly close to her own questioning hazel ones.

"What brought that up?"

"Watching you today. I've never had the opportunity to observe the lovely Senator Eve Meredith Steele at work. You really care, don't you?"

"I do," she agreed softly. A slight sigh escaped her lips as she cupped the glass, warming the dark amber liquid in her hands. "Sometimes, perhaps too much. It's impossible to do everything."

"You have a problem tilting at windmills?"

"I've been accused of that."

"Not one of your critics could ever say you aren't pragmatic when you have to be, Eve. Look at your investment program. And your arts-relief measure. A true Don Quixote would want the state to hand over the money to bail out the flagging film industry. Your idea of selling bonds to fund new projects created in California with California labor is far more practical. And much more likely to pass, since the general population doesn't feel as threatened by bonds as it would by additional taxation."

He smiled, a crooked, self-deprecating smile as he shaped her shoulder with his palm. "I'm man enough to admit when I'm wrong, Eve. You've got a great mind on those beautiful, tense shoulders."

"Thank you, Alex." Eve was surprised. One of his more furious arguments in Mexico had been that women such as she had no business in politics. "Such as me? And exactly what kind of woman am I?" she had shrieked at the time.

"The decorative kind," he'd shot back in a blinding rage, "appealing in public and satisfying in bed!"

It was then that she had slapped him and stormed out. She hadn't seen him again until he'd shown up here five days ago.

An errant thought tried to make itself heard inside her head. Was Alex's sudden appreciation of her career nothing more than the regrouping of his forces? Was he planning to attack from a surprise vantage point?

"Would you think I was staging a frontal assault if I took this blasted tie off?" His voice sliced into her troubled thoughts.

Eve closed her mind to the irksome problem, reaching up

to tug at the knot of the striped tie herself, slipping it off and placing it on the table in front of them. She felt his indrawn breath when her fingers touched him. And she knew that if she had an ounce of sense, the time had come to call it a night. But she remained, as though rooted to the spot, exchanging a long, silent gaze with him.

She couldn't voice a single word of protest when he put his glass down on the table before taking hers deliberately from her hand and placing it beside the first. Eve didn't say a word and she didn't move. Not toward him. But neither did she move away. She only waited for the inevitable.

# Chapter Five

"Eve?"

Her name was emitted on a deep groan a moment before Alex drew her gently to him. Eve gave a soft, almost sad little murmur of acquiescence, surrendering her last shred of resistance. As her arms closed around his neck, Alex felt the passions that had been stored in his body these long, lonely months spark and catch fire. Even as he felt himself overcome by the powerful reactions she produced within him, Alex forced himself to go slowly, carefully.

His lips moved over her face lightly before covering her slightly parted lips. The moist tip of his tongue crept into her mouth, evoking from her that strange, pleased sound he hadn't been able to banish from his mind.

Her breasts rose and fell rapidly, taut against her gray blouse, and Alex hurried to unfasten the buttons while her own hands, in turn, were busy with his shirt. Her nails traced a path across his chest, moving in slow, seductive circles through his crisp, black hair.

"Oh Eve . . . my sweet bride . . ." Alex dragged his lips away from hers, moving in a burning path to explore the hollow of her throat. The gray silk blouse landed on a chair halfway across the room and his hands moved to her shoulders, slipping aside a lacy strap of her camisole. His lips brushed her pearly skin before moving both straps down her arms, and Eve shrugged out of the pale lilac confection, granting him welcome access to the satin skin of her breasts.

Eve's hands clenched his muscled thigh as his mouth closed on her breast. He suckled with increasing need as his tongue swirled about the cherry-pink crown, creating a warm rush of sensation. Every female instinct in her body was rising to a high pitch as his warm lips nuzzled her fragrant skin, savoring the sweet taste of her.

Reality faded into the distance as she felt herself being lowered onto the satin brocade sofa and she pulled him with her, her hands running frantic trails up and down his back.

"Whatever other problems we may have, you can't deny that we were meant for each other in this way, Eve." Alex's voice was hoarse.

No, she'd never be able to truthfully deny that only in his arms had she discovered true fulfillment. Only Alex Steele had the capability to reach down and draw out the sensual woman he had discovered dwelling deep within her cool exterior. She writhed under his touch, her hair spreading over the pillows like honey.

Eve felt his knee coaxing her thighs open and she granted access, her hips lifting slightly off the sofa to meet his slow, erotic fingers as they slipped under the linen skirt and silky slip to trail sparks along her nylon-clad thigh. The maurading fingers were unkindly impeded from their quest by the tight mesh of her pantyhose.

"This is killing me," Alex groaned, his thrusting hips driving her deeper and deeper into the ivory satin. "Let's go upstairs. Please, love. Just let it happen. Let me be good to you . . . Let's be good to each other."

She shook her head wordlessly, her actions belying the denial as her hips moved in sensuous circles against him, her hands pulling him into her with an overwhelming need.

Eve felt a stab of pain as he suddenly drew back. "Then come swimming with me."

His smile was beguiling, his words a silken trap. Eve knew it. She could spot the ruse as easily as a cunning fox could spot a snare in the forest. During their brief time together, their late-night swims had often been the only time their busy schedules coincided. Choosing not to waste precious time talking, they'd invariably ended the night making love. While they hadn't learned much about each other's inner feelings, their bodies had retained no secrets.

Eve watched Alex's full lips curve in satisfaction as she emitted a small, quivering sigh of surrender, relenting to the truth of their mutual need.

"Just a swim," she said shakily, both of them knowing that her words could not be taken seriously.

Alex's eyes flamed, and his lips covered hers in a long, lingering kiss, drugging her with their warmth.

"Just a swim," he echoed.

Taking her hand, he drew her up off the couch and Eve stumbled, finding that her legs would not support her. He slipped his arm about her waist, holding her against his hip as he led her to the French doors that opened onto the terrace. An automatic timer had turned on the landscape lights surrounding the jeweled beauty of the pool and the enticing scene greeted them as they stood together, bathed in a muted glow. The lights played on the water and a gentle breeze skimmed the surface, creating delicate ripples. The stone fountain at the end of the pool whispered a soft murmur as the water trickled down the dark stones.

Alex held her in the circle of his arms, gazing down into her uplifted eyes for a very long moment. His eyes were deep wells and Eve felt herself being pulled into them, as if she were drowning in the warm ebony depths.

"I think John Wayne, after all," she whispered softly into the fragrance of the night air.

"Why?" Alex's knuckles brushed her cheekbone, moving to follow the smooth line of her uptilted jaw.

"It must be World War II we're recreating here," she explained as her own palms cupped either side of his head. "I feel as if I've been cast in the role of the kamikaze pilot."

There was a shadow of pain in his dark eyes and his mouth curved sideways in a rueful smile.

"No, Eve, I promise. I'd never let you destroy yourself in this little war of wills. Never that!" he whispered fiercely.

His eyes narrowed for a timeless heartbeat of a moment, capturing hers in an intense stare. Dark eyes asked, then coaxed, then softened with a gentle promise. Luminous hazel eyes faltered, then trusted, finally answering with slumbrous invitation.

Eve watched as his mouth approached her lips, refusing to consider whether what she was doing was wise or not. That mattered not at all. At least, not now.

Piece by piece, the rest of her clothing fell to the flagstones as Alex undressed her. Her skirt and the wispy bits of lace were covered in turn by his own clothing. Eve shivered in delightful anticipation, thinking as he drew her body into his hard, aroused length, that he would bring an end to this sweet torture.

But instead, Alex loosened his hold on her, walking with her to the shimmering pool where he led her down the curving steps into the warm, velvety-soft water. He floated on his back, pulling her with him, his hands spanning her slender waist and, as long as they both flutter-kicked, Eve found she could be towed easily. Her breasts lightly bounced against his chest and her lips met his with light, nibbling kisses. The motion of their legs caused their hips and thighs to meet and part, the uncompromising maleness of him brushing with teasing regularity against her. Neither one could give in to the full, flaming range of emotions without going under the water, and Eve wondered how something could be both so pleasing and painful at the same time.

Finally Alex brought her to the spa in a curve of the pool. With delicate, fluttering strokes, Eve ran her fingertips over his body, delighting in the way she could arouse him with her increasingly intimate touch.

His dark hands moved over her, his square nails scoring her flesh lightly as they moved up her thigh.

"Oh! . . ." As his teasing, tormenting fingers reached the warm juncture of her legs, Eve cried out his name in a weak, ragged sigh.

"I've got to have you, Eve. All of you," he groaned from deep in his chest as he drew her closer so she could feel the proof of his undeniable need. "Please don't fight me tonight. I've never been so hungry for a woman as I am for you. God, I've missed you!"

Eve trembled at the passion in his voice. She dug her nails into the smooth skin of his back, drawing him nearer. She felt as if her body had suddenly flamed, like a fireball of oil blazing atop the water. She could feel the physical waves pulling at her, washing away all pretense. Only to look at him, in the iridescent sapphire light of the pool, brought her pulse to a fevered pitch.

"Please, Alex . . . Love me." Her hands left his back, circling to run across the taut skin of his stomach, down the dark wet arrowing of hair, creating a tremor she could feel through her fingertips as he responded to her intimate caress.

"Is this a surrender, Eve?" His hoarse voice rasped against her mouth, but he held his body just out of reach.

Eve knew that if either one of them were to put a stop to this before the ultimate consummation, she would probably wither up and die right here. Every nerve ending was screaming for his touch and, although she thought she had experienced the pinnacle of lovemaking, her desire for him had never equaled this. Yet her pride managed to flare for a brief instant, like the final, fatal gasp of a candle.

"Not surrender," she whispered, twisting under the devastation his fingers were creating as she moved her hips closer to his probing touch.

Eve felt his soft sigh mingle with her own heated breath. "All right, then, love. We'll settle for a cease-fire. For tonight."

Alex finally moved between her thighs, filling Eve with an aggressive, elemental male strength that claimed her very soul. She gave a soft cry of delight as she wrapped herself around him, drawing him into her feminine softness as they were enveloped in a jeweled sapphire womb. She felt herself caught up in a swirling eddy of passions, overwhelmed with a warmth that swelled and cascaded like the water moving over them.

"Alex . . . I'm drowning . . . Alex!" Nothing had prepared Eve for the flood of passion resulting from her barren life without Alex these past months and there were no words to describe what was happening to her as she tumbled into a whirlpool of primal need.

"Don't worry, sweetheart. I'll take care of you. Trust me." As if to allay her fears, Alex turned her in the water, allowing her the physical support of his strong body as his hands cupped the curves of her hips, pulling her down onto him with a power that disintegrated the last vestige of Eve's self-control.

Something shattered inside her with all the violence of a bursting dam and she was consumed in hot, churning waves, her breathless cries smothered under his thirsty mouth.

Alex's deep, possessing thrusts ceased for a moment, allowing Eve the full blaze of savage rapture. Then, as if fed by her wrenching response, he moved against her with increased rhythm, reclaiming what he'd branded his that night under the stars, as they'd lain surrounded by wild-flowers.

Eve held him to her for a long time, savoring the stolen sweetness of his presence. For the moment, all the tense hostilities had been washed away and she was content to lie in his arms as the soft, warm water lapped gently over them.

"Eve?" Alex was filled with hope that their love-making would lead to a total reunion, but some basic instinct made him cautious. He was afraid to shatter the blissful, languid mood.

"Yes, Alex?" she murmured, still floating sensuously on the golden aftermath of pleasure.

"Don't make me sleep alone any longer. Please come back to our bed."

A cease-fire, a temporary truce, was one thing. But total surrender was an entirely different story. They both knew Alex held a devastating weapon in his arsenal; more than anything in this world, Eve loved the touch and taste and feel of this man's strong body against hers.

Like an alcoholic drawn to the bottle, she was drawn to Alex Steele. Over and over. And, just like that alcoholic, now that she'd slipped off the wagon and sampled this sweet turmoil, it would be even harder to evade his touch the next time.

It had taken every ounce of strength she'd possessed to rebuild her life after that horrible argument in Mexico. That blow had been followed by the illness that had culminated in her miscarriage. Her probable infertility had left Eve feeling like an empty shell of a woman, the agony made all the more painful by the fact that she had been forced to face it alone. Eve didn't think she had the strength to go through it all again. This man, while devastatingly appealing, was far too dangerous. Getting involved with Alex again would be like holding a stick of dynamite and walking into a room full of pyromaniacs.

Alex recognized her dilemma and forced himself to be patient, a virtue that was alien to every fiber of his being. His deep voice sliced into her unhappy thoughts. "I won't press you for an answer tonight, Eve. You've had a long day. But promise me you'll give it some thought. Whatever problems we have to work out, sweetheart, you can't deny that we're very, very good together."

No. She'd never been able to deny that. Alex was so very special to her. But was she really that special to him?

"It's never been like this with any other woman, Eve," he vowed with a flare of heated passion, as if he'd read her mind. "I swear it. Keep that in mind while you're making your decision."

Abruptly he rolled over, pulling her back into deep waters. They went under the surface, legs and arms entwined, and as they slowly rose, his mouth coaxed hers into blissful response.

"Race you to the steps," he challenged, as they broke the crystal-blue surface, taking off with strong, smooth strokes.

Eve shot after him, gasping as she drew herself up to where he waited on the top step.

"You cheated!" She choked as she rubbed the water out of her eyes with her fingertips.

"Of course. But I won."

"You always do, don't you?"

"Cheat? Only when necessary. Win? Of course." There was nothing playful in his tone as he rose from the pool, the water running off his body. "Come on, sweetheart, it's your bedtime. Am I invited to run with you in the morning?"

Eve ran her eyes up and down his hard body, delighting, against all her stern injunctions, in his sheer male strength and vitality.

"Think you can keep up?"

"Have I ever let you down? I've never heard you complain about my stamina." Alex gave her a buccaneer's grin, which caused her body to flush with renewed desire.

"Never," she answered softly. Not in that respect, anyway.

Alex rose from the water, scooping up their scattered trail of clothing. "You've gotten quite messy, Mrs. Steele, leaving your clothes all about like this. I hope you haven't learned any other bad habits while your husband was away."

"And if I have?"

"It may take time, but I'll simply have to get to work breaking you of them. Beginning with that handsome aide you've encouraged to take over your life."

Eve felt a cold shiver that wasn't a result of the night air. "Barry hasn't taken over my life, Alex, but he is indispensable. I need him. And, I like him."

"Do you love him?"

"Of course not!" The answer flew off her tongue automatically. What a stupid question! How could she possibly love Barry Matthews when she was so completely, horribly in love with Alex?

Oh, God. She was. Eve had been refusing to accept the treacherous thought, believing that Alex was out of her life forever. But one's heart didn't always listen to logic. The thought played over and over in her mind as she felt an instant stab of pain behind her right eye and her hand flew up instinctively.

"Migraine?" Alex's arrogant tone softened immediately as he recognized her response.

Eve could only nod, the headache crashing down upon her, nausea beginning to rise in her stomach. He scooped her up into his arms, carrying her against his damp chest through the house and up the long stairway.

"Alex." She tried to complain when he entered their bedroom. No, she corrected herself through the pain, his room now.

"Hush, sweetheart." He pulled back the comforter and slid her between the celery-green satin sheets. "I just want to take care of you. Where are your pills?"

"I don't have any," she moaned, remembering that she'd planned to stop by the pharmacy Monday afternoon. But Barry had thrown that newspaper at her, effectively banishing everything but Alex Steele from her mind.

"Do you want me to call the doctor?"

"No. I just need some sleep. I'm sure it'll be gone in the morning."

Alex studied her, an atypical expression of hesitation furrowing his dark brow. Making a decision, he left the room and Eve could hear water running in the adjoining bathroom. Moments later he returned with a cool, damp cloth that he placed over her eyes.

"Here you go, sweetheart. Try to relax."

Eve experienced a brief moment of panic as the nude male body slid between the sheets, and Alex drew her to him. But his fingers were content to brush light caresses against her temples and his voice crooned soft, sweet words into her ear. Under his gentle touch, Eve allowed her body to melt against him in remembered bliss, then she drifted off to a peaceful sleep.

A pale yellow beam of light was peeking through the narrow opening in the draperies, teasing Eve awake. She kept her eyes closed, testing to see if the headache was gone. As she became assured that sleep had banished it, she also became aware of another presence in the room. Opening her eyes slowly, she saw Alex standing beside the bed.

"Good morning. How's the head?"

"Fine," she acknowledged, looking up at him. "You've been running."

Her sleep-hazed eyes swept over him, taking in his athletic frame, tee shirt and shorts. A filmy sheen of perspiration glistened in the morning light against his dark skin and, try as she might, Eve couldn't turn her eyes away. Alex possessed a vitality so palpable it reached out and touched her even as she fought to conceal the familiar reaction stirring within her.

"I didn't know when you'd wake up," he explained. "And I didn't think you'd be up to exercise."

"I'm fine. Thanks."

"Good."

There was a little pool of silence. This is an uneasy truce, at best, Eve mused, realizing in the light of day that both of them were searching for a safe middle ground. It was almost as if last night's shared ecstasy had not eased the tension, but complicated it.

"Oh. I brought you your juice." Alex thrust it out rather self-consciously, like a teenage boy giving a girl a corsage before their first prom.

No Heathcliff, John Wayne or Cary Grant this morning, she thought, falling into Alex's movie game. A young Jimmy Stewart, perhaps. The idea of Alex cast in such a sweet, harmless role made her smile.

"You're going to spoil me," she replied lightly, reaching for the enticing orange juice.

"I'm going to do my damndest." That's all he'd ever wanted to do, Alex thought, give Eve his world and everything in it. But she possessed her own maddening ideas of independence. He had sat up most of last night, watching her sleep, reliving scenes of their past that flashed before his eyes like a late-night movie. He'd hoped that last night had meant as much to Eve as it had to him, but by her cautious behavior this morning, Alex realized that of all the battles he'd fought in his life, this one was not only going to be the most difficult, it could also be his first failure. That bleak idea gave him a pang of bitter disappointment and he was swept by a mood of discouragement. The dark expression crossing his face banished the brief glimpse of vulnerability. Then he abruptly turned away. "I think I'll take a shower."

Eve could hear the water running and her mind's eye conjured up a vision of her husband's lean, strong body as she'd experienced it last night. A fleeting shiver danced down her spine and she swallowed the last of the juice in a fast gulp, scolding herself for being so damn susceptible to Alex Steele. Just because the man had the ability to shake a woman to her toes didn't make him a good husband.

Alex reentered the room, a short emerald towel tucked around his waist. There were drops of water in the ebony and silver waves of his hair and as he sat down on the mattress beside her, Eve's senses were enveloped by the familiar musky scent of his after-shave. His brief display of anger had vanished and he reached out to brush tousled waves of dark honey hair back from her forehead in soothing strokes.

"Are you certain it's all gone?"

"I'm sure. Thank you for taking care of me last night."

Alex had stopped stroking her hair and was bracing himself with a hand on her pillow as he leaned over her, his dark eyes an intriguing mixture of concern and desire. Fighting against succumbing to any enticement, Eve moved her gaze down his rugged features, seeking a safe spot to fix upon.

His straight, uncompromising nose led directly to the black fringe of his mustache and her mutinous mind and body conspired to recreate the sensation of the short, soft hairs against her skin. Continuing downward was certainly no help. There she was faced with those chiseled lips which promised, and delivered, all sorts of sensual delights. Even his thrusting chin was home to a deep cleft, one she had loved to feel under her fingertips as her own tracing fingers explored his face so many times in the past.

She couldn't contend with the rock-hard chest, where the lush pelt of jet hair led down to arrow into the soft emerald terrycloth. Alex was too much of an assault to the senses first thing in the morning. What she wanted, more than anything in the world, was to turn the clock back. Before today. Before Mexico. Back to their honeymoon, where she could be free to reach out and pull him down to her.

The migraine had come like a lightning bolt out of a clear blue summer sky. But he had been the cause, and nothing to do with Alex Steele had ever given her a moment's warning. Not that first, overwhelming surge of desire he'd stirred in her, not their quick elopement or her unplanned pregnancy. And certainly not his return from Europe to this house. Everything about him had always kept her off-balance. Something that was alien to her well-structured, well-managed life.

Alex reached out to trail his hand along her cheekbone, moving down her throat and across her delicate collarbone. His eyes gleamed with a lazy heat as he finally answered her statement.

"Taking care of you last night was a pleasure, Eve. In every way."

Stung by what she considered to be sheer male arrogance in his voice, Eve gathered up her cool composure. She'd known last night was going to prove to be an enormous mistake. She'd only let her defenses down for that brief, passionate interlude, but like a centurion set on conquest, Alex had stormed her parapets and was now firmly entrenched in his enemy's camp. Ben-Hur? Lawrence of Arabia? El Cid, she decided.

"Don't get any wrong ideas about that," she responded in an even, restrained tone, worlds from what she was actually feeling. "It only represented a little sexual relief. I've been busy campaigning, and my work doesn't come with the obvious perks yours does."

Damn her. Eve had grown up in the business. She knew that most of the rumors of location affairs were nothing but media hype. Alex knew she was using those stories to dodge the real issue between them.

The muscles bunched tightly in his jaw as a thin white line circled his lips. "You're just going to keep it up, aren't you, Eve?" She could feel his contained energy as Alex struggled to keep his temper. "You just won't give up the fight."

"I told you," she reminded him firmly, "I have no

intention of surrendering to your ridiculous campaign to worm your way back into my life. We made a deal and I'll stick to my part of the bargain. But," she added, gaining renewed strength, "the moment the polls close, I expect you out of here."

"Don't I even get to hang around for the results on channel seven?"

"There can only be one result for us, Alex. And that's been determined. I've already voted."

"Ah," he retaliated swiftly, "but I haven't."

Venom hardened her hazel eyes, cloaking the still-painful memories as they stared at each other aggressively. "Oh yes you did," she flung back. "You voted in Mexico!"

A soft oath flew off his tongue as Alex leaned forward, gripping her shoulders.

"You're going to stay right here in this bed while we get that out of the way. Once and for all."

Eve could feel the force of his fury flowing into her from his fingertips. His keen black eyes showed a dangerous ferocity and a flood of heartfelt relief washed over her as the bedside telephone rang, slicing through the tense atmosphere.

"Let it ring!" His demand was harsh, but inexplicably desperate. She refused to consider the reason and, with a defiant shake of her head, reached out and picked up the receiver.

"Hello? Oh, Barry." She forced her shaky tone into one of warm welcome. "I'm glad you called. I'm running a little late this morning, but I promise to be at the office soon."

She forced a provocative laugh at something he'd said, causing Alex's face to darken perceptively. "Now, now, Barry, don't even suggest such a thing." She laughed silkily into the phone. You *should* have been an actress, she thought, watching Alex's face as the conversation progressed.

"You know I can usually get up in time by myself. I certainly don't need you to come over and pull me out of bed."

Eve forced another bubble of warm laughter, watching through lowered lids as Alex left the bed. She kept making soft, friendly comments into the telephone, hoping she was still answering at the proper times. In truth, she was hearing little of what Barry had to say. Instead, her surreptitious attention was entirely on Alex, who'd decided it was time to change tactics.

She would have expected blistering fury, but Alex now appeared unconcerned about the interruption as he unpeeled the green towel from his dark body. His back was to Eve, but the effect was devastating as she watched the waves of muscle narrowing from the wide wedge of his shoulders down to his lithe waist. A slim band cut a swath across his tanned body, displaying the mark where his brief swim trunks had covered his lean buttocks.

Silky briefs and then a pair of cream-colored jeans were lazily pulled up over his legs. Next came a scarlet silk shirt that he left unbuttoned for the moment. He returned to the bed and the mattress sagged under his weight as he pulled on socks and a pair of calfskin boots. Eve belatedly realized that his disinterest in the feigned sparkle of her conversation had been a ruse, as he leaned toward her.

His long dark fingers pushed back her tumbled hair as he murmured into her ear, his breath a warm caress. "Not bad, sweetheart," he growled with a seductive, rolling brogue. "If I ever do a remake of *Gone With the Wind*, I'll keep you in mind for Scarlett. Especially that scene where her husband carries her off to bed in order to teach the vixen a well-earned lesson. How many takes do you think it would take to duplicate Vivien Leigh's satisfied smile on your gorgeous face?''

He winked with a blockade runner's arrogance and Eve realized that she was indeed looking at Rhett Butler at his most rakish. As Alex watched the recognition dawn, he grinned, his teeth a slash of white under the panther-black mustache.

''Ouch!'' The exclamation spilled out as Alex took a playfully vicious nip on her earlobe.

''Eve? Are you all right?'' Barry's voice reinsinuated itself back into her consciousness.

''I'm fine.'' Eve's eyes threw daggers at the man who was chuckling as he made his way to the door. He turned, his dark eyes dancing with unrestrained glee as he posed with male arrogance, preparing his exit line.

''Oh, Eve?''

She covered the mouthpiece with her hand. ''What?'' she snapped, knowing full well he'd wait until she accepted her cue.

''Unlike that other scoundrel, my dear, I really *do* give a damn.''

Alex blew her a brief kiss and vanished from view, the taps of his boot heels muffled on the thick carpeting of the hallway. Eve sank back onto the pillows, a defeated expression furrowing her brow.

''Eve? Are you still there?''

''Yes.'' She heaved a great sigh. ''Barry, would you believe that, at this moment, I don't give a damn whether California runs out of water or not?''

She held the receiver away from her ear as her aide began an almost hysterical tirade. God, she was getting tired of men this morning. And it was only—she glanced at the clock radio—nine o'clock.

"All right, Barry. I'll be ready. Yes, I'll pack a bag so we can stay over. See you soon."

She'd no sooner hung up the phone than it rang again.

"Hello? Oh, hi, Dad." Eve knew the lack of enthusiasm was evident in her voice, but here was one more member of the male species she didn't feel up to fencing with today.

"I'm sorry it was busy. I was talking to Barry." Eve inhaled a quick breath. "Oh, Dad. I did forget. I've had such a weird week. The party's tonight?" She pursed her lips in frustrated irritation as one more male began making demands on her.

"Look, Dad. I've got a meeting in San Francisco on water allocations for the south. I don't think I'll make it back in time."

His staccato voice rang in her ear like bullets. "I understand it's an important affair, Dad. But some people might argue that water is important, too. We can't all live on imported champagne, you know."

Eve sighed as the verbal barrage continued. "Dad . . . Dad! Wait a minute. Why can't Natalie act as your hostess?"

She was naming the latest of her father's constantly changing companions. The man changed women like he changed cars, she thought. It seemed to be a Hollywood pastime. Musical beds. Eve had seen enough infidelity in this town to have made a vow at an early age to avoid marriage altogether. Something she'd succeeded in doing quite nicely until she met Alex.

Again the rapid-fire missiles. "Dad, listen to me. Dad? Let me get a word in! It's not my fault you're not choosier in your playmates. Just keep the liquor away from her and she'll be fine."

The insistent male tone on the other end of the line gave way to a teary, imploring female voice.

"Yes, Nat." Eve nodded, her hazel eyes growing bleak. "I know it's hard. He's always had enormous parties like this. I know you try not to get scared. Oh, damn it, Natalie, put him back on."

She drummed her fingers on the satin sheets as she waited, hearing the sobbed request on the other end.

"Look, Dad, I'll do my best, but I'll probably be late. Do you think if Natalie knows I'm coming, that will be enough? Can she stick to ginger ale for an hour or two before I arrive?"

Eve listened to the explanation she'd heard too many times before, nodding her head automatically before she cut in.

"Okay, Dad. See you tonight. Oh, I'll probably be bringing Barry, if we get back too late. I'll take my dress with me and come to your place straight from the airport." Her shoulders slumped in defeat. "You're welcome. I love you too, Dad."

Eve had been serving as her father's hostess for the elaborate parties the head of Olympus Studios liked to throw since her sixteenth birthday, only a few weeks after her mother's death. Since her parents' marriage had become only one of economic and social convenience, the untimely crash of the sporty Mercedes convertible which took her mother's life hadn't seemed any reason to call off a party that had been months in the making, Jason Meredith had argued.

However, the lack of a proper hostess had been an irritation. Until Eve had been given another long look. Her father had been too busy over the years to take time to observe his only child's growth. But when she arrived home from her Swiss boarding school for the funeral, it took only a single glance to see that she'd matured into a charming young woman. She'd possessed an air of poise not acquired by many individuals in a lifetime. Drafted into service, Eve filled the role so well that she was promptly enrolled in a private high school in the city, so she could continue to add the feminine touch Jason felt was vital to his social occasions. College had been the University of Southern California, keeping her close at hand.

A problem had developed over the years as Eve became more and more wrapped up in her own life and responsibilities. Jason had a long-time penchant for becoming involved with young actresses who'd never lived the sumptuous life-style the man preferred. A party for five hundred could send almost anyone into a tailspin, and the latest resident of the Meredith mansion had discovered, to everyone's dismay, that a handful of Valium, washed down with a bottle of French champagne, did a lot for the nerves. Unfortunately, it hadn't done much for the party when she'd pushed a diplomat from an oil-rich country into the pool after he'd suggested she return to the Middle East with him—as the latest acquisition to a happy household that already boasted four wives.

Eve put the brakes on this line of thought as she glanced at the clock. Barry would be here in a few minutes. As she washed her hair in the shower Eve considered, not for the first time, that too many people expected too much from her. There was her father, and Natalie, and Barry. And those ghostlike images that hovered in the pockets of her mind: her constituency. A group that never spoke with a united voice, yet somehow expected her to satisfy all of them. An impossible and frequently wearisome task. And now, with Alex back, bringing along a new set of demands, it looked as if things were only going to get a lot worse before they got any better.

# Chapter Six

"Wow! Too bad we can't use that get up for your posters. There isn't a man in California who wouldn't vote for you looking like that!"

Barry's eyes were bright with male appreciation as Eve emerged from the cramped lavatory of the private jet her father had dispatched to fly her back to Los Angeles. As a rule, she flew on commercial planes, tourist class, but Jason Meredith had given orders to the pilot that she was to be flown out of San Francisco the moment she left her meeting.

Eve ran her hands down the white silk crepe Grecian-styled gown. "Thank you," she smiled wanly. "I'll tell you, Barry, I sure don't feel up to this tonight. After the day we've had, I just want to go home, put my feet up and listen to some soft music. Then, after a couple glasses of wine, go to bed."

"Now that's the best idea I've heard all day. Why don't we just do that?" He gave her a guileless smile.

"Terrific," she said dryly, not taking him seriously. "I'm sure Alex will be delighted to leave us alone to neck on the couch."

"There's always my place." His low tone held a note of

encouragement and Eve studied Barry's face for a hint of his usual teasing. To her private dismay, she couldn't find it.

"Barry . . ." she began hesitantly.

He rose from the chair, crossed over and put his hands lightly on her shoulders, brushing her cheek with his lips in a friendly, nonthreatening kiss.

"Don't worry, Eve. I've opened the wine. Why don't you pour us a couple glasses while I go change? Although I totally agree that there are far better ways to spend this evening. I don't know why I agreed to go with you to Jason's little carnival in the first place."

Eve patted his smooth cheek with her palm, bestowing a warm smile upon her friend and associate. "Because I can always use a friend when I'm being thrown into that sharks' tank."

"Ah, but there are those out there who would accuse you of bringing along your own shark, Eve."

Her hazel eyes grew sober. "I know. But you've never been anything but good to me, Barry. And I always make my own judgments about people."

Eve felt her breath catch for a brief moment when it looked as though his full, sensuous lips were about to lower to hers. She knew her apprehension must have shown in her eyes, because Barry pulled back, a crooked smile of chagrin on his handsome features.

"I'd better get ready."

She nodded. "I think that's a good idea."

When he left, Eve opened her compact to study her features judiciously. She'd known for some time that Barry's feelings for her went beyond that of a usual working relationship. She also realized that he'd demonstrated uncommon patience, apparently willing to wait until her marriage was legally dissolved before declaring himself.

Barry would remain a sterling example of propriety, Eve decided, if for no other reason than to protect a career they'd both worked hard to build. They'd been through a lot together; wasn't it possible that in the heat of the campaign Barry had mistaken a strong love of friendship with that between a man and woman?

She sighed, not finding the answer in the small circle of glass which reflected her pensive image, and put it away as Barry rejoined her.

"You look exceedingly handsome, as usual." Eve smiled, holding out a glass of chilled white wine to him. He did look good. Barry was tall and muscular, with wide shoulders and a narrow waist that the expertly cut evening clothes only enhanced. His thick, wavy golden blonde hair was a foil for the bronze of his California tan and his sparkling gray eyes were the color of finely buffed pewter. Yes, a good-looking man. A *great*-looking man, Eve corrected herself. But he didn't stir one tiny, feminine sensation within her. She sighed.

"You *are* tired." Barry joined her on the small couch in the passenger area of the sleek jet.

"Exhausted," Eve agreed, taking a sip of the crisp Chablis. "Barry, do you think we accomplished anything today?"

"I think so, Eve. But we'll know better when we get back to the office and can assimilate that mountain of data."

She put her feet up on the table in front of her, disregarding the high-heeled gold sandals she wore. If her father was going to drag her back to L.A., when she'd much rather be up to her neck in bubbles in a tub at the Hyatt Regency on San Francisco's Embarcadero, then he could darn well live with footprints on his walnut tables.

"It's such an age-old problem. The argument never

seems to change. There are times I think California might as well be two separate states."

"It's been suggested before," he agreed, putting his arm along the back of the couch in a casual gesture. "Remember, back when cross-filing was allowed, there were stronger political rifts between the two areas than there ever were between parties."

She sighed once again. "I know. And after reapportionment gave us more seats in the senate, we've been seen as an ever-increasing threat. There are times when I attend meetings that I feel just like a carpetbagger entering the South after the Civil War."

"It's a major problem," he acknowledged. "But the fact remains that sixty percent of California's population lives in the dry southern areas, Eve. Anyone can see that something's going to have to be done to ensure a continuous supply of water for us."

She ran her finger around the rim of the glass thoughtfully. "I know. But I can understand how the northern residents feel, too. They're up there with all the resources and as far as they're concerned, we're just greedy hedonists, filling up our swimming pools in Lotus Land."

It seemed so simple, in theory, she mused. The northern area's forests preserved much of the state's precious water supply. So, all that had to be done was to take the rain and snow runoff from the north and move it to the arid locations of the south, where it was needed. But the crux of the matter was that no one had ever really figured out the most equitable way to do that. Then, too, Oregon's constant, almost paranoid fear that California was after all its water added further complications.

"You know," Barry reminded her, "the SWP has done a lot of good with all the dams, reservoirs, aqueducts and power plants. It may just be time for the folks up north to get used to the idea."

Eve knew all the arguments in favor of the California State Water Project, but she could list off the top of her head an equal number of problems with the project that directed fresh water out of the San Francisco Bay and Sacramento Estuary area for use in the south.

Dwelling on these matters, Eve thought, not for the first time, how lucky she was to have Barry for a sounding board. He understood her. Understood the importance of her work. Her father, caught up in his beloved studio, never had appreciated her choosing politics as a career. And Alex—well, Alex was right in line with Jason Meredith, as usual.

"Don't forget," she replied, "if I can play devil's advocate for a moment, the SWP has continually fallen short on the promised water delivery. And you can't overlook the fact that it's decimated fisheries and polluted northern waters. And with that," Eve sighed heavily, lifting her glass to her lips, "we're right back to square one. I wonder who the good guys are in this water war?"

Right now, she couldn't begin to answer her own rhetorical question. The northern groups had brought in all their experts today, citing the cost of more growth of the water project as well as environmental concerns. The southerners had just as many authorities, including their own environmentalists, who'd forecasted drought and economic ruin for southern California, which would affect the entire state. It would take a modern-day Solomon to determine an outcome that would satisfy everyone.

Eve glanced out the oval window, seeing the long landscape of sparkling lights that signaled their approach into the Los Angeles area. She put her glass back in its rack and fastened her seatbelt for landing.

"Well, first thing tomorrow, I'll start trying to make some sense out of all those notes I took. Then I'll do the only practical thing."

"What's that?"

Eve grinned at Barry, deciding to put the problem out of her mind for the rest of the evening. "Pray for rain."

Barry presented their invitation as he was stopped at the tall iron gates, flashing it at the guard before continuing up the long, curving drive to her father's house.

"I don't believe this!" His eyes opened as wide as silver dollars as he pulled up to the area designated for valet parking. Leaving the keys in the ignition, he got out and went around to open Eve's door, but was denied the chivalrous task by a tall young cossack clad in a scarlet tunic, black pants and high glossy boots. Opening the door with a flourish, the young man bowed deeply as she stepped out. Then, after handing Barry a claim check, he slid behind the steering wheel and drove the car away.

Every tree on the grounds had been strung with tiny white lights, filling the night with bright, twinkling stars.

"Leave it to Daddy," Eve murmured as they strolled arm-in-arm toward the sounds filtering over the soft night air. Laughter, music, a raised voice now and then—all the strains of a successful party in full swing. "If the L.A. smog won't let the stars shine for his party, he'll play a B-version God and turn on his own."

"What the hell is that?"

In the distance there was an enormous building that looked totally incongruous in the Beverly Hills neighborhood. The structure rose high into the night sky, a profusion of disparate exterior designs that were uniquely medieval Russian in content, form and feeling. The eight onion-shaped domes gleamed from various, well-placed spotlights.

"Why Barry," Eve chided with a crooked grin, "don't tell me you can't recognize St. Basil's Cathedral?"

"Of course," he returned instantly. "I was just a little surprised to see it transferred from Moscow to California. What happened? Did it defect?"

"Olympus Studios is doing a remake of *Anna Karenina,*" she explained. "This," she waved a hand, encompassing the elaborately decorated grounds, "is the official announcement."

"It's a good thing your constituency can't see the way you live, honey," he mumbled as they stood surveying the brilliant scene before them.

"I don't live this way," Eve reminded him.

"I know. But you know what they say about the sins of the fathers—" He stopped again, his mouth dropping open at the sight before him. "Let me guess."

"Go ahead." Eve replied with overt amusement.

His gray eyes were sweeping across the huge structure, which encompassed enough space for a football field. The unmistakable exaggerated Renaissance form of the baroque Winter Palace, home of the czars, was a masterpiece of architectural drama, even scaled down as it was. The sweeping curves, columns and arches were detailed down to the last pilaster, including the tall statues along the top of the massive structure.

"The Winter Palace at Leningrad."

"St. Petersburg," she corrected lightly. "This all takes place before the revolution, remember? The name hadn't been changed yet."

"Now I understand the revolution," he murmured as they approached the waiters in swallow-tailed coats manning enormously long tables laden with a vast assortment of foods.

"Barry, dear," Eve twinkled up at him, "you're seeing capitalism at its finest." She grimaced slightly as she noticed the huge, baroque fountain that was gushing forth vodka instead of water. "And perhaps its worst," she agreed.

"The Winter Palace is in St. Petersburg and St. Basil's is in Moscow," Barry pointed out, his analytical mind rejecting the pairing of the two massive structures.

"Literary license. They're the two most recognizable and elaborate works of Russian architecture Dad could come up with." She laughed at the incongruity of their conversation. "Besides, how could you possibly demand a semblance of realism from a scene that's sheer fantasy in the first place?"

He laughed. "Got a point there, Senator."

"Eve! Am I ever glad to see you! How was your trip, darling?" A tall, ebullient man with swept-back silver hair strode toward her, his arms open to enclose Eve in a bear hug.

"Just fine, Dad. Thanks for the plane."

"No trouble, honey. I was eager to get my best girl here as soon as possible. You know the party can't start without you!" His bright blue eyes scanned her, parental pride competing with the gleam of the spotlights brightening the palace. "You look stunning, as usual. Absolutely stunning. I never could understand why you insist on being a politician when you could easily be the most beautiful actress on the screen."

"We haven't all been bitten by the movie bug, Dad," she laughed. "I'm fully vaccinated against it and I make sure I keep my booster inoculations current."

There was a roar of appreciative laughter as Jason

Meredith waved an arm. "Well, what do you think?" His sapphire eyes were bright as he awaited her review.

"It's unbelievable, as usual." Eve smiled with genuine affection for her father. "I really am amazed that you were able to create this thing. How many set designers did you *borrow* from the studio?"

He wagged a finger at her. "Now Eve, you're the one who's constantly preaching about the need for more work for those people. With the industry down right now, you should be thanking me. In some countries I'd probably receive a medal for assisting my country."

"In some countries," she teased, "the peasants would be getting ready to storm these gates." She cast her eyes upward, encompassing the facade of the palace. "It *is* magnificent, though."

"Well, it's not as large as I would have liked. The original is five hundred feet long and three hundred and eighty feet wide. Held sixty-five hundred people. Imagine." Jason looked as though he was allowing himself a private fantasy before he held out his hand toward Barry.

"Good evening, Matthews. It's always good to see you."

"Thank you, sir. It's always a pleasure to be invited." Barry had slipped on his professional mask of courtesy. Eve knew he liked Jason Meredith as an individual, admiring the drive and power of the man who'd single-handedly created an empire, but the opulence of his life-style had always been a source of concern. Barry worried that Eve would someday be tarred with the brush of the conspicuous consumption that her celebrated father enjoyed so openly.

"I think you were born in the wrong era, Dad," Eve laughed. "You would have loved to live in this palace."

"Probably," Jason agreed cheerfully. "But I can assure

you I wouldn't have enjoyed being the last resident. That's what I love about America. Instead of wanting to drag you down to their level, the poor are just waiting until they can join you on yours." His cobalt eyes lit suddenly as he spied a movement beside him.

"Oh, Nat, darling. Come and say hello to Eve." His arm reached out and pulled an extraordinarily beautiful young woman to his side.

"Hi, Eve." The woman's dark eyes were warm and grateful.

"Hi, Natalie. Quite a party."

Eve smiled, noting that Jason had obviously dressed Natalie to enhance his party theme. The low-necked black velvet dress exposed her porcelain shoulders, even more noticeable due to their ivory complexion. She must have been keeping out of the sun for weeks to obtain that fair skin, Eve mused. The dress was richly trimmed with fine Venetian lace, which looked as if it had been dipped in a strong tea. Her hair was piled on her head, dark ringlets escaping at the temples and nape of her neck. Her arms were full of bracelets and a single strand of pearls echoed the gleam of her skin, a perfect adornment for the black velvet gown. There were small clusters of pansies at her waist and in her hair, the yellow faces of the purple-black flowers seeming to smile their approval.

Anna Karenina, the night she fell in love with her handsome Vronsky, Eve noted, admiring her father's innate flair for the theatrical.

"You look ravishing, Nat." Eve smiled sincerely, thinking that despite her slight nervousness when faced with all Jason's elaborate productions, the woman had a sweet vulnerability about her that was endearing. Of all the women her father had lived with over the years, Eve liked Natalie the best. And felt the sorriest for her. Unlike so many of the others who'd come and gone, Natalie seemed to have the misfortune of being in love with the man. She would undoubtedly be hurt when he moved on. It was as if he got his women from central casting, Eve thought, not at all charitably.

These days, his pet project was *Anna Karenina*. So, he'd gone out and found himself an Anna. Next year it could well be Amelia Earhart. Or Aimee Semple McPherson. And Natalie would be on her way out the ever-revolving front door.

"Thanks, Eve. It was Jason's idea."

Eve's smile deepened. "Yes, I thought it was."

She took Barry's arm. "Come on, Barry. Let's get some of that food before my stomach starts echoing like the cannons signaling the start of the revolution."

"Eve, may I speak with you a moment?" Her father's tone clearly indicated he preferred a private audience.

Barry patted her arm. "I'll fill a couple plates and meet you over by 'Swan Lake.' " His blond head nodded in the direction of a small pond that was home to a pair of regal-looking swans.

"Thanks," she agreed.

"Eve, you should probably know this." Jason Meredith had a guilty look on his face, like a little boy caught with his hand in the cookie jar.

"Oh, what did you do this time?"

"Alex is here."

Her eyes flew to his face and she paled considerably. "Oh, Dad," she groaned. "Why did you do that?"

"In the first place, I've always liked him. In the second place, it would look damn odd if I hadn't. The man's just back from Europe, Eve."

"Believe me, Dad, I'm well aware of that."

"His presence would have been missed and tomorrow

morning we'd be reading in all the columns that *Heaven's Rage* is expected to be a bomb, because I refused to let Alex in my home. Besides,'' he added crankily, ''the man *is* your husband.''

He was out of line there, Eve thought. Since when had her father begun worrying about her personal life? But he *was* right about one thing. The industry worked under a microscope; too often the slightest irregularity was blown totally out of proportion. If the early word got out, however mistaken, that the movie Alex had directed in Mexico was in trouble just a few weeks before distribution, it would almost guarantee a self-fulfilling prophecy, giving Alex his first box-office failure.

''Don't worry, Dad. It's a big party. I probably won't even run into him.''

''I knew you'd understand, darling.'' He dropped a quick peck on her cheek before leaving her to greet a Japanese shipbuilder.

''Problems?'' Barry looked up from his smoked salmon as Eve sat next to him.

''Not really. Alex is here, that's all.'' She looked down at the plate Barry had prepared for her. ''My goodness, you did take me seriously about being hungry!''

The large plate held melon and Parma ham, crepes stuffed with generous pieces of king crab, some sliced breast of capon and the obligatory caviar.

''I wonder if this is actually Russian?'' she mused, eyeing the caviar.

''I wouldn't doubt it. Another thing your voters could hang you for. I can see it now—SENATOR DINES ON RUSSIAN DELICACIES WHILE MILLIONS GO JOBLESS.''

Eve laughed, a light, silvery sound. ''You worry too much, Barry.''

"Well, I *am* worried about Alex. I'll admit that. What are you going to do about him?"

Eve stalled for time, taking a sip of the wine Barry had brought for her, thankful he'd passed up the vodka.

"Are you asking as a friend or a political advisor?" she asked finally.

"Can't I be both?"

Eve looked out over the pond, observing the two swans, their question-mark necks twisted together into an intricate black-and-white puzzle.

"We've proclaimed a truce, of sorts," she murmured.

"Why?" The single interrogative was harsh, sounding like a bitter oath.

She turned her soft hazel eyes back to his face. "Because he's already done the damage with that article about our reconciliation."

"He *did* plant that story. I knew it!"

"He did. But if I throw him out now it will make me look ridiculous. And, even worse, indecisive. Tell me, Barry—as a political advisor—how many people do you think would vote for a senator famed for her vacillation?"

"So. It's just one happy little family?"

"Not exactly. He's promised to move out as soon as the campaign is over."

Barry's high, smooth forehead gathered into thoughtful lines. "That doesn't make any sense. What does he hope to gain from the few short weeks left in the campaign?"

Eve felt the color rise into her cheeks as she toyed with her fork, her eyes cast downward.

"I see. This is just an excuse to remain in the house until he can seduce you back into line, right?"

"Barry!" she hissed, glancing around to see if anyone had overheard his raised voice.

Consummate political tactician that he was, Barry dropped his tone immediately. "Well, isn't he?"

"Don't be silly."

"Have you slept with him yet?"

Eve shot him what she hoped was a killing look. "I don't believe that my relationship with my husband is any of your business, Barry." She turned her head away, hoping to escape his probing gaze, and her eyes ran into disaster.

Eve would have recognized that strong, straight back anywhere. Just as she would have recognized the curling little ebony hairs that were brushing against his snowy white silk collar, the little crisp hairs that some feminine fingers were twirling in as they played with them. The couple was swaying to the haunting strains of the violinists, and as he swung her around, Eve watched her husband laugh at something the woman had said.

A stabbing pain forked through her, and with it came the excruciating realization that she was jealous. Eve didn't know who the woman was, but at this moment, she wanted to yank her hands off Alex's neck and throw her bodily into the pond, where she could damn well drown among the lily pads.

What in the world was wrong with her? Why should she care what Alex did? Or who he danced with? Only a few days ago, she'd been counting the days until he was out of her life.

"Eve?" Barry's concerned tone recaptured her attention. "What's wrong?"

Eve shook her head, smiling a wobbly little smile. "Nothing. Come take a walk with me?" She rose abruptly, her movement almost overturning the small table.

"Sure." He put his hand lightly on her back as they

strolled away from the noisy confusion of the party into a grove of tall trees.

"What's the matter?" Barry turned, spanning her slim waist with his hands.

"Nothing."

"Eve, I thought I was your friend."

Her shoulders lifted and dropped as she breathed deeply. "You are, Barry. A dear friend. But this is a problem I've got to work out by myself."

"It's Steele."

Eve lifted misty hazel eyes to his probing study. "Yes. It's just that everything's so confused."

"Not really, Eve. Just remember how the bastard treated you after Mexico. Is that how you want to spend your life?"

"No." It was a whisper. She thought of Isadora Meredith, left at home while Jason devoted his entire life to Olympus Studios. His only daughter had been shipped off to boarding school and his wife quietly remained in the background, serving a decorative function as she put up with his work. And his other women.

Eve realized that Alex had expected the same from his marriage. Hadn't he called her a "decorative type" of woman during their final, heated battle? Hadn't he wanted her to give up her work and live her life through him, gratefully accepting whatever time and energy he was willing to toss her way? No, Eve could never live that way.

"No," she repeated, a bit more firmly.

"Then the solution is to divorce the guy. Now. Just as you'd originally planned."

"But the campaign—"

"Hang the campaign!" Barry exploded with unaccustomed anger. "You were a damn popular senator before you met the guy and you've built a popular political base all by yourself. Your career doesn't hinge on him. Hell, honey, this is California. Everyone has a divorce or two in their closet. They're not going to get uptight because you made a little mistake with your personal life."

"I don't know—" God, why was she so ambivalent all of a sudden?

"I do. Trust me. Haven't I always known what was good for you? Haven't I always been right?"

His fingers cupped her chin, lifting her troubled gaze to his as his other hand stroked her back in a comforting caress.

"I suppose so."

Eve was not surprised when the kiss that had been retracted earlier on the plane returned, covering her lips. She was also not surprised when nothing wonderful happened. It flashed through her mind that if she could only experience something from this, achieve some sort of responsive emotion, she could learn to ignore the chaos that Alex was capable of creating in her. She lifted her arms around Barry's tanned neck, allowing him to draw her body into his. Eve closed her eyes, willing some spark, some rush of feeling to occur. One finally did, but it was not Barry's doing. Once again, Alex was the cause.

"Well, this is a cozy little scene."

Eve's arms flew from Barry's neck and her head spun in the direction of his maliciously mocking voice. Barry held her calmly in the circle of his arms, not appearing in any hurry to release her.

"Well, well, so it's true what they say. Speak of the devil and he always shows up."

"That's right," Alex answered, his voice a silky smooth threat Eve had learned to recognize. It was an interesting contradiction about her husband, that the quieter his tone was, the more dangerous his mood. ''I'd suggest you take your hands off my wife, Matthews. That is, unless you want that pretty face of yours messed up.''

''Alex!'' Eve found her voice. ''Please don't create a scene.''

''I was under the impression that the two of you were busy doing just that,'' he drawled laconically. ''You're just lucky I found you instead of one of the members of the press who are always skulking about these little social functions.''

He'd obviously brought reality crashing back into the encounter, Eve noted, as Barry's hands dropped away. Alex had successfully located the chink in her aide's armor.

''That's much better.'' Alex's midnight black head nodded his approval. ''Now, Matthews, why don't you go find yourself some nice, agreeable lady to bestow those kisses on, while my wife and I join the party?''

''She came with me, Steele.''

Barry seemed determined to stand his ground as long as he could without creating a scandal, and Eve watched the animosity spark between the two men like static electricity. There was a battle of wills occurring here and she could almost hear the clash of swords.

''There was a time, Matthews, when you'd have been invited out to the dueling grounds for compromising a man's wife.''

Eve broke into the conversation, deciding the time had come to call a halt to this archaic behavior. ''That's ridiculous, Alex, and you know it. I think making that Victorian novel into a movie must have gone to your head. This is the twentieth century. Men don't fight duels over a woman's honor any longer.'' Her hazel eyes flashed as she glared up at him, offended by his possessive attitude.

''Oh no?'' he challenged, crossing his arms over his

chest and looking down at her. He seemed to have forgotten Barry's existence as his attention was captured by Eve. "And what, exactly, do twentieth-century men do, love? Stand by and allow other men to carry off their wives?" His jet eyes glittered treacherously. "Not this man, Eve. You may consider me under the influence of my movies, even a throwback to the Dark Ages, but I believe in love and honor. And protecting what's mine."

"Yours?" She gasped, her eyes widening with incredulity. "I'm not *yours,* Alex. I'm not any man's." Her hands were splayed across her hips, her aggressive stance contrasting with the Grecian femininity of the dress. "So, why don't you just go back to whomever you were dancing with and leave me alone!"

"I've already told you, Eve. I'm not leaving you here with Mathews. Can't the two of you get that through your heads?"

Eve put her hand on Barry's arm, feeling his muscles tense as his hand clenched. She realized that both men were coming incredibly close to reverting back to more primitive means of solving this age-old dilemma, and knew the fallout from such behavior would be devastating.

While it would virtually finish her campaign chances, it wouldn't do a lot for Alex's career, her father's party or the delicate-natured Natalie. She hated to back down, but Eve reminded herself that discretion, after all, was the better part of valor.

"Go ahead and have a good time, Barry," she suggested softly, patting his taut forearm. "I'll be fine."

His eyes were like cold steel as they raked across Alex before his gaze returned to her. "What time shall I take you home?"

Before Eve could open her mouth, Alex interjected an answer. "I'll be taking my wife home. Isn't that the way it's usually done?'' He held out his hand. ''Eve, are you coming?''

She watched Barry stalk away, rage in every long stride. ''Why do you do things like that?''

''Like what?''

''Act as if you own me when he's around?''

''Simple. Because he wants to, and I don't want him to get the wrong idea.''

''That's ridiculous!''

''Is it?'' He looked at her, his eyes the color of a robust cup of coffee. ''Look, Eve, we have an agreement—for better or worse. There's no room in our life or our bed for an extra man.''

''You've definitely found your niche in creating fantasies, Alex, because you've got one terrific imagination.''

''Don't you see anything? The man's in love with you, Eve. If I let you divorce me, Matthews would propose in two seconds flat. And, like a fool, you'd probably marry him on the rebound and end up miserable. I won't allow it.''

They'd been walking back to the party and Eve stopped suddenly. ''You won't *allow* it?'' Her voice rose as she turned to face him. ''*You?* You have nothing to say in the matter, Alex Steele!''

''I do for now,'' he contradicted her blandly. ''You're stuck with me for the next few weeks. If I can't convince you that you're making a big mistake by then, well—''

''Well what?'' she inquired suspiciously. ''Don't forget, there's more to that agreement.''

As Alex started to reply, they heard Eve's name being called. Turning, Eve saw with dismay that Rhonda

Simmons, the well-known gossip columnist, was walking toward them.

"Put a pretty smile on your face, darling," Alex whispered in her ear as he smiled himself, "it's time to mingle for Daddy."

# Chapter Seven

The smile Eve had pasted on her face felt frozen as they finally escaped the party. She leaned back against the leather seat of Alex's black Lotus, glancing over at his firm, dark profile beside her.

"Who was that woman you were dancing with?"

Alex turned his head, his enigmatic gaze searching her face. "Why?"

Eve shrugged. "I was just curious."

"Do you care?"

"Of course not."

A laugh rumbled from his chest, deep and warm in the intimate confines of the sports car. "I don't know how you can be such a good politician, Eve. You're a lousy liar."

"Not all politicians lie!"

"And you don't?"

"No. I do not."

The husky chuckle rumbled again. "I know. I was just teasing. And, although you don't care," his drawling tone was laced with amusement, "she was the wife of a banker who happens to be a major financer of *Heaven's Rage*."

"How nice that you've got such cooperation from both

members of the family,'' she observed dryly, hating the woman even more.

''It always helps. Just like you seem to get such cooperation from your staff. May I remind you, I was only dancing with the lady. What you and Matthews were doing out in the bushes was a bit more intimate. I would suggest, my darling wife, that this is a case of the pot calling the kettle black.''

''That was the first time I've ever kissed Barry.''

''I see.''

''It was!''

''And I said, I see.''

''And there won't be a second time.''

''Didn't you like it?'' There was a suggestive grin teasing at the corners of his mouth under the black mustache as he turned his gaze toward her for a brief moment. The light dancing in the jet depths of his eyes was irritatingly devilish.

''Alex,'' Eve's voice was a low warning.

''Don't bother to answer, Eve. I told you that you wouldn't like making love to that shark. And, I suppose, in a way I'm even glad it happened. Gave you a chance to discover the fact for yourself. That's the only reason I didn't break his jaw. It just didn't seem worth it.''

''You think you know everything, don't you?'' Eve glared at him furiously, but his attention had returned to the darkened roadway. The same roadway, she realized suddenly, that they'd taken that first night. Sunset Boulevard.

''You know, I enjoyed the last time better.'' His voice was low and vibrating, laced with silky seductiveness. He'd read her thoughts once again.

''Oh, Alex . . . Please don't . . .''

''Remember? You were wearing a sea-green chiffon

gown that matched the color of your eyes in the moonlight after we'd made love. I don't think I'll ever forget those beautiful, misty green eyes. God, you were lovely!"

Eve turned her attention to the dark shadows flashing by her passenger window. There was a huge, painful lump in her throat and she swallowed, attempting to dislodge it. She closed her eyes as Alex rested his right hand lightly on her leg, as if it had every right to be there.

"I think it was right about this spot," he continued, "that I knew we'd never make it straight home. The touch of your fingertips on my skin felt like a brand. I thought I'd claimed you when I walked into that party, Eve. But in reality, you'd claimed me. I was just too filled with my own male ego to see it then."

Eve didn't answer as she fought against the flood of sensuous memories. Why didn't Alex stop this? Didn't he realize how much those memories hurt? The good ones were even more painful than the bad—they reminded her all too vividly of what they'd lost.

They fell silent and after a time he pulled the car off the road, cutting the engine. He rested both forearms on the top of the leather-covered steering wheel, gazing out through the windshield into the black night.

"Let's talk."

"No." It was a weak, whispered protest.

"It's time, Eve. We have to work this out and put it behind us."

"I want to go home."

"Not yet." Alex turned around, reaching behind him. "I've still got the blanket." There was a grin curving his lips but Eve thought she saw a flash of regret in his obsidian eyes.

"There's nothing to discuss, Alex."

"On the contrary," he returned, refusing her soft protest. "There's a great deal to discuss. Your life, mine, ours."

Eve watched as he went around the front of the car, opening the door for her with a silent but forceful attitude that she decided not to put to the test. She didn't protest as he took her hand and led her down the narrow path.

"Just a little stroll down memory lane," he murmured.

She waited silently as he stopped and spread the blanket out, then sank to the ground beside him.

"I wanted that baby, Eve," Alex began without preamble.

She started to get up. "If you're going to continue to lie, Alex, this is a waste of time."

His hand moved with the speed of a striking cobra, encircling her wrist and holding her to him.

"It's no lie. I'm guilty of being incredibly stupid, an overbearing, class-A jerk. But I've always loved you, Eve. And I never meant to hurt you like that." His words caused goose bumps to rise on her skin and Eve shivered slightly.

"Cold?"

"No."

Alex took off his dinner jacket and slipped it around her shoulders. Eve inhaled deeply, filling her senses with the aroma of musk that mingled with his own masculine scent.

"Do you want the entire story? Or the condensed version?" he asked.

"I don't want any part of it."

"That's illegal."

Her attention swung to his enigmatic face. "What do you mean?"

"As one of the august members of the legislative branch of our government, you should know that I'm entitled to a fair trial before you can find me guilty."

''All right,'' she sighed, willing to give him that.

''When you arrived, the shooting was already running two weeks behind schedule.''

Eve nodded, remembering well. ''The monsoons were early.''

''That's right. We were losing every afternoon to those damn rains. The temperature, if you'll recall, was in the hundreds, the humidity almost as high. It was like trying to make a movie in a steam bath and everyone was ill-tempered and edgy.''

Her eyebrows arched. ''Don't tell me you're going to blame all this on the weather?''

Alex's fist hit the blanket. ''No, damn it. But Lori Ireland was becoming impossible to work with. She was crying and carrying on and I'd been watching her getting closer and closer every day to a complete breakdown. I *had* to finish that picture. On time and under budget.''

''Always the picture first,'' she murmured, remembering her father's devotion to his work.

''Almost always,'' Alex corrected, remembering the ineffable sense of loss and loneliness he'd experienced when Eve's divorce petition had been served to him on the set. ''There was a lapse from the show-must-go-on commandment in England. But that's another story you chose not to believe.'' There was a harsh tone roughening the deep voice, but he continued.

''When you showed up in Mexico, I'd been wondering just what kind of marriage I'd rushed you into. I'd wanted to be a different kind of husband, Eve. To make a different type of family. But there I was, hundreds of miles from my wife, and far worse off than I'd ever been when I was single. Because I knew what I was missing. I lay awake nights, watching the damn cockroaches climb those filthy walls, trying to figure out how we could carve any personal time for ourselves out of our individual rat races."

Eve looked into his face, which was shadowed in the moonlight, doubt etching deep furrows between her hazel eyes. "Are you trying to tell me that the great and powerful Alex Steele is actually admitting he's less than perfect?"

A muscle jerked in his strong jaw. "Sounds a little incredible, doesn't it?"

"That's the word. I don't believe it. And I can't believe you actually expect me to. You acted like some type of nineteenth-century male chauvinist, insisting I give up my career just so I'd be available for you whenever you found the time to come home."

How could he love her so and still want to wring that beautiful neck?

"I'm sorry," he shot back, his tone harsh. "I'm damn sorry that I was enough of a throwback to consider our child something special. But I hadn't had the time to consider the matter with your analytical expertise, Eve. It was, after all, a bit of a surprise. There'd only been the one time we hadn't taken precautions."

"Here," she murmured, stroking the blanket with her palm.

"Here," he agreed roughly. "I thought I was going to die when you left Mexico. And when you had the abortion, it was as if you'd killed me all over again."

Eve shook her head as an icy fear engulfed her. Alex couldn't possibly think the loss of their child had been a deliberate act? But if he did, her wildly spinning mind realized, that would explain his months of silence. In fact, if that was the case, she was amazed he didn't hate her. But here he was, professing his love.

She took a deep breath, venturing into dark, unknown

territory. "Alex, you don't think that I . . . Alex, I was sick. I wanted that baby more than anything. Especially when I thought everything was over between us. He was the only thing left of our love. But they couldn't save him."

Oh God, what the hell had he done? How much damage had he caused by leaving her alone, licking the imagined wounds of his damaged male pride? Alex realized once again that this reconciliation might be more than even he, with all his determination, could bring about.

Eve watched his dark face blanch as confusion reigned on his moonlit features. He covered his face with his fingers, and she felt like weeping as a strange, choked sound came from his throat. When he finally lowered his hands, the eyes which held her gaze to his were as bleak as a tomb.

"But I called the hospital as soon as I could find a phone after your father's telegram arrived. Some nurse told me you'd had an abortion and had been released."

A bell rang, clear and loud in her head. "Oh, Alex. It was a miscarriage caused by my illness. I loved our baby."

As I love you, she added mentally. She wanted to fling herself into his strong arms right now and put everything back the way it was. But was it too late? Had they caused each other too much pain? She sighed, her exhaustion returning as she tried to face this new predicament.

Alex heard the slight breath, realizing that they were both exhausted and the idea of the misunderstanding was too new and raw to deal with rationally right now. He held up his arm, reading the dial on his watch in the silvery moonlight. His voice was unusually flat, but Eve noticed that it no longer held the grievance it had earlier.

"God, it's late. And you probably had another one of those killer days. Why don't you cancel everything you've got planned for tomorrow and we'll spend the day working our way through this maze we've gotten ourselves into."

"Do you think we can?"

Eve wondered if his suggestion would only serve to open her up to more pain. She loved Alex. She always had. But that had not been enough to protect them both from an incredible amount of grief. How could love be such a devastating thing?

"We can try. I know it'll hurt a lot less if we finally talk about it. Remember, I promised not to hurt you this time."

"I've got so much to do," she hedged. "The campaign, the water issue, the arts-relief measure—"

Eve knew Alex could feel her weakening as his hands moved to massage her neck and shoulders in the seductive motion that never failed to soothe.

"Play hookey with me, Eve. Please?"

She turned, her face a scant six inches from his. "Please? That's not a word you toss around, Alex."

"You're right," he agreed readily, his hypnotizing fingers continuing their sensual magic. "I save it for important things. Like now."

His dark eyes were like two beckoning fingers as he enticed her further. Eve closed her own eyes as her head moved to his, her lips lightly grazing his. His tongue just penetrated the sweetness of her mouth with its sensual tip and Eve's lips softened and parted, inviting it further.

As the kiss lingered, Alex savored the delights she was offering. His lips created a bubbling effervescence in her veins and Eve could feel her heart beat against his chest with all the snappy cadence of a snare drum. This was what she'd hoped to find in Barry's kiss. This wellspring of pleasure that only this man—her husband—could instill in her.

Eve felt a flash of regret as his hands went to her shoulders and he put her a bit away from him. "It's late," he murmured. "And we have a big day ahead tomorrow. Today," he amended. "Let's go home, Eve."

He rose and Eve took the downstretched hand he offered. Alex held the blanket under one arm, the other curved around her waist as they headed back up the moonlit path toward the car.

"Wait."

Eve stopped at his softly issued command, watching as he bent down and broke off one of the long-stemmed, black-faced flowers. He slid it into her hair, then, placing his palms on either side of her face, gave her a long, lingering kiss. She turned her lips into his palm as the kiss finally ended, then her hand snuggled back into his as they continued on their way.

"I want to swim some laps before bed," Eve said as he pressed the remote-control button to open the garage door.

Alex looked at her with disbelief. "At this hour?"

"I didn't run this morning. Besides, I'll sleep better."

He shook his head. "I thought *I* was an exercise fiend. You, my darling, are an absolute Spartan." His teeth flashed in a friendly, easygoing grin that told Eve he wouldn't argue the point.

She experienced a glimmer of hope. They were becoming much more relaxed in each other's presence and the aura of distrust seemed to have been banished by the discovery that they'd suffered equally from the loss of their child. At least now they were no longer working at cross-purposes.

"Well, if you want a fat wife, Alex . . ."

His eyes burned with a smoldering approval as they took

a leisurely inventory of her body, enhanced by the clinging white crepe gown.

"You could never be fat," he avowed. "But if you insist, I'm not about to turn down an opportunity to see that gorgeous figure in a bathing suit. Do you mind if I play spectator tonight, instead of participant? Unless you'd like company?" His husky voice vibrated with a surge of masculine desire.

"You can cheer me on," Eve suggested, smiling tentatively.

Alex took the rejection without issue. "I'd love to."

They walked hand in hand into the house and he headed into the dining room. "I'm just going to get a little brandy while you change," he said. "I'll meet you out by the pool."

He was already lying in a lounge chair, his shoes off and his shirt unbuttoned, when Eve arrived, clad in a scant white bikini. His smile of greeting tugged on her heartstrings. It looked so natural, so unforced, as if he, too, could feel the static slowly disintegrating from the air between them.

Eve entered the soft warm water with a graceful dive from the side of the pool and began swimming smooth, even laps. Twenty minutes later, she pulled herself onto the cantilevered decking, feeling like a new woman. The exercise had worked out all the knots of tension and banished the heavy pall of exhaustion that had been overwhelming her.

Alex was instantly by her side, wrapping a huge soft towel around her shoulders and putting a brandy snifter into her hands.

"I love to watch you." His deep voice was smoky and soft in the perfumed night air.

"Swim?" Eve's eyes smiled her thanks as she took the glass.

"Swim, make speeches, anything. Everything. You have no idea how much I've missed you, Eve."

"Yes, I do." She trembled slightly at the thought of how many nights she'd longed for him by her side, willing to forget the pain he'd caused for just one moment of the ecstatic pleasure they shared.

"You're never going to make it through the rest of this campaign if you don't start getting more rest," he ordered lightly, mistaking the cause of her slight shiver. "Without meaning to sound like an overbearing husband, I think you should get to bed."

Eve was caught in his deep caramel gaze for a long moment, like a butterfly in a net. "I think you're right," she agreed softly.

Alex held her hand lightly in his as they reentered the house, stopping at the top of the stairway.

"Which room?"

More than anything in the world Eve wanted to sweep the past behind them and join Alex in the wide, comfortable bed. But they'd already proven that sexual compatibility was not a strong enough foundation on which to build a workable marriage. She needed much more, and while she possessed renewed hope for their chances, she couldn't revert back to the beginning in one fell swoop. As much as they both wanted and needed each other, understanding and trust was important, too. She could only hope tomorrow would bring that about.

"I think the guest room," she answered, turning down the bright invitation in his eyes.

Alex took it without any sign of resentment. He entered the room, unplugged the clock radio and tucked it under his arm. Brushing a chaste kiss on her forehead, he advised, "Sleep as late as you want, Eve. We've got all day."

Eve slept soundly, not waking until the persistent rays of the brilliant California sun had been tickling her mind for some time. She propped herself up on one elbow, looking for the clock radio, before remembering that Alex had taken it away last night.

Last night. A reminiscent smile of pleasure curved her lips as she remembered. She hadn't wanted to attend her father's party. And she'd wanted to be there even less when he'd dropped that loaded bombshell about Alex's presence. But now, she was overwhelmingly grateful. She felt lighthearted for the first time in a very long while. Giddy as a schoolgirl, she was looking forward to their day together.

Eve had not taken a day off in ages. In fact, the last time had been her hospital stay after losing the baby. She'd always worked hard, but the past months it had been as if she was trying to bury her heartache in the demands of her political career. It had been a devastating year, costing her both her child and her husband. She'd locked the pain away, covering it with the glossy veneer of a chic, capable politician.

Today she would be spending time alone with her husband, gathering up those cold, scattered ashes of their marriage and seeing if it could be salvaged. And, for the first time, Eve felt there was a chance. Alex had been right last night. It was time to move on. Even the thought of dealing with their stormy past gave her no fear. Today she felt absolutely intrepid.

She ran a brush quickly through her sleep-tumbled hair, washed her face and brushed her teeth, then slipped into a blue satin robe. Following the enticing scent of freshly brewed coffee downstairs, she went in search of her husband.

"Good morning."

She returned Alex's welcoming smile. "Where's Mrs. Jacobs?" It seemed strange to see Alex moving around the kitchen he'd never spent any time in. Strange, but nice.

"I sent her to her sister's in Glendale for a nice, long visit," he grinned devilishly. "I hope you don't mind, but I wanted the house to ourselves today. All to ourselves." Again he flashed her that devastating grin.

Eve laughed, gratefully taking the cup of coffee he held out to her. "You sound exactly like a teenager who's just discovered his parents have to go out of town overnight, leaving you with the place to yourself. Are you planning a party?"

"A private one," he answered. "You know, that's exactly how I feel. I was beginning to think that the only way to get you off by yourself was to kidnap you."

"That's a federal offense," she murmured, taking a sip of the strong, hot coffee.

"Then I'm glad it didn't come down to that," Alex replied lightly. "Because I would have done it. This is an all-out, damn-the-torpedos battle campaign I've got going here, sweetheart. And speaking of that," his voice dropped a full octave, "since I seem to have my adversary in my sights . . ."

Alex took the coffee cup from her hand and placed it deliberately on the counter. Eve's eyes opened wider with anticipation, a sparkling emerald invitation. As he propelled her into hard, intimate contact with him, Eve experienced an erotic shock at the sudden impact, having expected something gentler. But then she could feel her adrenaline begin to flow as her answering desire flamed. The fire licked along her veins, devouring everything in its path as she flung her arms about his neck, pressing against his hard, taut body.

"Oh, Eve. How can you deny us this?" Alex groaned against her lips, his mouth devouring hers with insatiable hunger, drinking her essence with the gratefulness of a thirst-parched man coming across a sparkling oasis in the desert.

His hands stopped their heated exploration of her body to reach down and lift her hips, bringing them into even closer contact. Eve felt his need and the knowledge fanned her own until she could feel herself slipping, headed toward the vortex of their passion.

His mouth swallowed her answering words, as if to deny her an opportunity to negate the raw awareness they had of each other. A shared need which, once again, was blotting out all other thoughts and feelings, like a thundercloud blots out a pale, storm-filtered sun.

As Alex rained little kisses all over her face, Eve twisted her head to recapture his lips in a long, searing interlude, her fingers digging into his hard shoulders as she steadied herself. A weakness was spreading through her body, leaving her legs feeling weak.

"I can't deny it, Alex. I do need you," she cried, as his hands untied the silken sash of her robe and moved to caress the warm curves of her body underneath.

"And I need you, love." Then his actions negated his words as he dragged his mouth away and retied the royal-blue sash. "But I need to talk even more."

"Can't we talk later?"

Eve's movements were blatantly seductive and she tugged his shirt free of his jogging shorts to allow her fingers access to the soft mat of hair on his chest. She could feel the quick tensing of muscles and the short intake of breath against her ear as her fingernails found and flicked at his hard, buttonlike male nipple.

Alex's eyes were the color of aged brandy and just as warm as he removed her hands, kissing the fingertips in turn, before feathering light kisses on her palms.

"We'll talk first," he said firmly, but with a heart-quickening smile. "Then, we'll have the remainder of the day and night for whatever else you can think up to do on your day off."

Her dark lashes flew open. "Day off! I forgot to call Barry." Distress entered the hazel eyes as reality threatened to destroy the cocoon of sensuality that had been spun about them.

Alex's strong hands feathered along the fine bones of her spine, as he drew her back to him. "I called him," his husky voice assured her. "It's all taken care of. Don't give it another thought, honey."

At any other time, if anyone had told Eve that she would have tossed away her workday cares with this facility, she would have denied it vehemently. But now, she capitulated instantly, gratefully, to the firm lips plucking gently at her own, the circling hands on her back moving down her waist.

"Want a picnic breakfast?"

Eve looked at him curiously. "All right. I'll go get dressed."

"No need. You're just fine."

She watched as he took some English muffins from the broiler oven and jars of orange marmalade and currant jelly from the refrigerator. Filling a thermos with the steaming black coffee, he then placed everything in a small wicker basket. Then, his hand on her back, he led her out the kitchen door.

"I thought we'd have breakfast with the birds this morning," he answered her questioning look.

The treehouse, she realized. Built by the previous residents of her Pacific Palisades home, the treehouse was actually a wooden platform nestled high in the branches of a huge oak tree, almost hidden from view. Eve hadn't paid a great deal of attention to it when she'd moved in.

"Ladies first."

She eyed dubiously the boards nailed into the trunk that served as a ladder.

"Don't worry. I've already been up here this morning. It's safe."

Eve climbed until she reached the lofty platform. He certainly has been here, she thought, her hazel eyes softening to a misty, gentle green. Baskets of black-eyed Susans flanked the perimeter of the platform, and the familiar blue-and-black-checked blanket was spread in the center.

"We seem to get along best in this atmosphere," Alex said with a hint of an apology in his voice. "I suppose you think I'm cheating again."

Eve shook her head, her eyes brimming with affection. "No. I think you're being incredibly sweet."

His dark eyes widened slightly at her uncensored declaration and a slow grin tugged at the corners of his lips, finally breaking into a full-fledged, brilliant smile.

"Breakfast first," he decreed. "Then conversation." A shiny, provocative glint brightened his eyes. "And then I refuse to be held responsible for any naughty ideas you might think up."

Eve sat with her legs crossed Indian-style on the soft blanket as he poured her another cup of coffee and spread the thick, sweet marmalade onto the crisp surface of the halved English muffin before handing it to her. They ate in quiet solitude, enjoying the light morning breeze ruffling the leaves around them, the flitting of the birds as they skittered among the branches and the whirring hum of a cicada secreted somewhere in the deep green foliage.

It was as if they were in a private world high up here, hidden away like this. Eve wondered idly why treehouses had ever been considered the province of children. She saw no reason why adults shouldn't have the opportunity for such bliss.

After a time, Alex packed away the breakfast things, lowering the basket down to the ground on a rope that was attached to a corner bracing.

"Now, let's get this overdue chat out of the way." His dark eyes held a firm insistence, but his expression was warm and encouraging.

Eve drew her knees up against her satin-clad chest, encircling her legs with her arms. "When I first got the news of the pregnancy," she began softly, looking out over the landscaped yard from her bird's-eye vantage point, "I'll admit I reacted a great deal like you. I worried about how I could find time to be a mother, as well as a state senator. And a wife. Something I still hadn't had a chance to try out, really. I never expected to find myself pregnant. I knew that one night was foolish, but who really believes things like that happen?"

Alex nodded, watching her thoughtfully.

"I always thought I wouldn't have children because of my career. I didn't want to be a haphazard mother, or ship them off to some convent boarding school. I spent two weeks pacing the floors of this house, wondering what I was going to do. And, it always came down to how much I loved you, Alex. I knew I couldn't help loving your child. So, I began working out options—household help, trying to figure out how I could commute more easily from

Sacramento to L.A.—all the nuts and bolts of the prospect. When I thought I'd come up with a workable plan, I decided I had to go to Mexico. I didn't want to tell you in a letter. And I couldn't call."

"No phones," he muttered.

Eve grimaced. "No phones. So, I took a chance and arrived on location with my news."

"I behaved outrageously," Alex said, with a healthy dose of self-revulsion. "And I'm not asking you to forget it. But I'd like to point out that you had two weeks to get used to the idea. I was in the middle of the goddamn Sonoran desert, drowning in monsoons and budget overrides."

"I know." Eve shook herself slightly to discourage the creeping depression she knew was capable of covering her like a thick blanket, smothering her almost to the point of suffocation. She lowered her forehead to her bent knees.

"How much do you know about me? About my life before *The Star Seekers?*"

Eve turned her head, resting her cheek on her knees. "Fact or legend?"

A twinkle brightened his eyes for a moment, at odds with his expression. "That bad, huh?"

"You've established yourself as quite a cult figure, Alex. It's inevitable that the real man would be swallowed up by his larger-than-life legendary counterpart."

"The real man is the one sitting here with you, Eve. The one who grew up in a firebombed neighborhood in Belfast, watching an overworked mother of eight spend far too many hours on her feet over hot ovens in the family bakery. I watched that woman put in eighteen-hour days, never having a moment's rest, splitting her duties between work and home. By the time I was sixteen, I was the last one living in the house and decided it was time she had some freedom. So, with my parents' reluctant blessing, I packed my bags and moved to London."

"That's awfully young to be on your own," she murmured, thinking how she had arrived in Los Angeles at sixteen, to be immediately swept into her father's flamboyant existence.

"I did okay. I got a job at a bakery, bought my first sixteen-millimeter camera and set out to teach myself how to make films."

Eve managed a smile, despite her unhappiness at their impasse. "I can see why you make such good copy, Alex. You're a real rags-to-riches story. I can almost imagine Olympus Studios releasing it for the summer audience."

"There was a lot of luck involved. You see, at first I wanted to be a movie star. But I couldn't find anyone I trusted to run the damn camera. Eventually, I found I had a knack for film direction. I seem to be better at telling others what to do than doing it myself."

Eve chose not to point out that one of the things Alex Steele excelled at was giving orders.

"You really do love your work, don't you, Alex?"

"Of course I do. Just as you love yours," he pointed out with a degree of insistence. She had the impression Alex knew where this conversation was headed and didn't like the direction.

"Sometimes, during the past months," she said softly, her eyes moving across his tightly drawn features, "following news of you was just like watching my father all those years. I was afraid I'd made the same mistake as my mother. I'd fallen in love with a man who was already in love with that huge, flickering silver screen."

"Do you still believe that?"

Unable to submit herself to his intense scrutiny, Eve shut her eyes, shaking her head in a weary motion. The only sound for long, heavy moments was the rustling of the leaves as the robins played musical branches in the deep green canopy overhead.

"I don't know," she answered truthfully. She lifted her distressed face to his, silently asking him to understand. "I never seemed to have time to think straight when I was with you. It was all so sudden."

"Like falling overboard into a storm-tossed sea," Alex said lightly.

"Exactly. How did you know?"

His mouth curved into a self-conscious smile. "Because I felt the same way. I knew I was rushing you, Eve. But I've already admitted to a bad selfish streak. I wanted you and I didn't intend to wait. But both of us were immersed in demands at work that didn't give us any time together. Then I had to take off for Mexico and everything went to hell."

"You really wanted my baby?" she whispered.

"*Our* baby. Yes, I did. You weren't the only one crying, Eve. Believe me. It tore me apart to think you cared more about your career than you did about establishing a family with me."

Eve shook her head. "I thought we could do both, Alex. I never made a conscious choice. I still think we could have made it work if we'd both tried."

"And you think I'm inflexible? Because I wanted to save you from the burden I watched my mother carry all those years?"

Eve watched as Alex methodically stripped apart a broad green leaf, shredding it unconsciously as he awaited her answer. It suddenly occurred to her that his intransigence had not been due to any real need to dominate her. Instead, he'd only been trying to make life easier for her. Comparing the strong woman who'd raised that enormous family while working in her husband's bakery with the convent-raised daughter of a wealthy man, it would appear that Eve might need to be treated like a piece of fine crystal. Alex had sorely underestimated her. But in their whirlwind courtship neither had spent a great deal of time truly learning to understand the other.

"There's a vast difference between working to put food on the table and working for the love of it, Alex," she said softly, putting her hand on his arm. "My career would just have made me a more fulfilled wife and mother." Eve's soft voice dropped to a low monotone, and she turned her head away, unable to meet the rush of emotion she saw in his gaze.

"If I stay with you, Alex, we won't be able to count on children."

He reached out to put his arms around her, resting his cheek on the top of her head. "I love you, Eve. I don't care if you can have children or not. I think the one thing we can both agree on is that we married without either one of us seriously considering the matter. And I'll admit that the one thing I've definitely learned from all this is that nothing is worthwhile if I don't have you to share it with. I put my life and my heart in your hands when I met you, love. The next move is yours."

Eve pulled back slightly, studying his intense features. "Oh, Alex," she whispered, "I've been operating on autopilot all these months, pretending to be a human being. But I've felt as if I were dying. You're the only man I've ever loved. The only man I want in my life."

Alex's strong features were oddly vulnerable as all the guard fell away from his eyes. "Mrs. Steele," his voice was shaky with emotion, "I'd say we've wasted enough time."

# Chapter Eight

Alex's hand slid under her thick hair, holding the back of her neck as his lips lowered to touch hers with a silky, exquisite touch. His fingers plucked at her robe and Eve noticed through her haze of pleasure that his hands were trembling ever so slightly as he bared her satiny skin to his touch. Her nipples gathered themselves into expectant little points, causing his eyes to glow with lambent desire.

Before, their lovemaking had been done in an atmosphere of cease-fire, the lull before yet another storm in their tempestuous relationship. But the mood was suddenly very different as both seemed willing to put the past behind them and seek a new direction for their life together.

"So much better," Alex whispered as his palms skimmed over her warming flesh and Eve knew he sensed the reincarnation of their marriage as well. Like the legendary Phoenix it seemed to rise from its own ashes, promising to soar to new and wonderful heights.

Her fingers moved to the buttons of his shirt, working them with an urgency that would no longer be denied. She pushed the burnished silk off his shoulders and was only vaguely aware of the garment falling to the ground below them like a gleaming bird.

Alex was tender as he lowered her down onto the blanket, settling himself alongside her. Eve could feel the crisp black hairs of his chest rubbing against the bared skin of her breasts and she writhed under him, the sensation creating havoc to her senses. His hand trailed down her slender throat, brushing along the bare flesh of her shoulder, his thumb massaging with featherlike touches along her collarbone.

"Oh, Alex." Eve's breath came in little gasps as she moved under him, wanting to feel his body against every inch of her smoldering skin. "I love you so very, very much."

His eyes were like burning coals, searing her with their kindled desire as her swelling breasts conveyed a firm and welcoming invitation. As Alex took an aroused pink tip between his fingers in a circling gesture, he created a warmth spiraling outward to spark along all her nerve endings.

"Oh!" Eve's soft sounds became a desperate cry when he repeated the sweet torture on her other breast, the answering heat in her lower body feeling like molten lava as it swept through her veins.

Alex's lips touched the rounded curve of her breast, his tongue trailing seductive circles, and Eve's fingers laced through his ebony dark hair as she pressed his head deeper into her yielding softness. She pleaded in whispered torment, no longer shy as she told each and every one of her needs and desires.

He gratified her every request, his teeth nipping at her sensitive skin, his short square nails scoring scintillating trails along her thighs. His lips followed the blazing, tormenting path, burning away coherent thought as he led her to the brink of oblivion at an erotic, leisurely pace. His warm, nibbling lips moved unhurriedly from her ankle, up the rounded firmness of her calf, along her thigh, taking tiny bites at the tender skin where her leg ended.

Eve arched in desperate response, her hips lifting off the blanket, but Alex lifted his dark head, only granting her a lazy, seductive smile. His nails grooved a trail back down her other leg, which was then treated to the same, agonizing experience. Once again when he'd reached the juncture of her thighs, he stopped and Eve cried out. Her cries changed to gasps as his tongue plunged, invading her feminine warmth.

"Alex," she gasped as his lips and teeth moved over her, branding every pore with their fiery warmth. "Oh my God . . . Please . . . Take these off . . ." Eve thrust her fingers between his warm, moist skin and the waistband of the frustrating barrier of shorts, reaching to brush across the hardness of his lower stomach. She could feel him shudder against her exploration and was rewarded when he stood up. His head practically brushed the green leaves overhead as he took off the shorts and briefs.

Eve reached up to him, her eyes welcoming him back to the satin warmth of her body. When he lowered himself to her, she moved against her husband, her hips dancing fluidly with his corded thighs. Her teeth bit lightly at his shoulder, while her tongue tasted the flavor of his glistening, damp skin.

"Eve . . . Oh yes." Alex groaned as she knelt on the blanket beside him, touching him without restraint, little snowflake caresses that had him growling deep in his throat. Her teasing touches feathered along his taut male body, her soft lips urging him to higher and higher planes of passion, until with a roar of agonized male demand, he pulled her into his arms, moving her onto her back. He covered her body with the flaming heat of his own, his hair-roughened leg parting her satiny thighs.

Her nails raked along his back as he moved against her and their bodies fused. Eve felt him move inside her, tensile steel warming her to her soul. He lifted her to him, holding her to his triumphant demands, but Alex's victory was hers as well and Eve clung to him, swept with a sudden weakness as they were flung through the universe, into the deep release of another world.

Then, for expanded, golden moments, the only sound was the twittering of the birds in the branches surrounding them and the whisper of the tranquil, soft breeze as it fanned cooling air across their skin. Eve's dark-blonde hair was clinging in moist strands against her forehead and Alex's fingers moved to brush it away, his gentle touch inexplicably more intimate than the tumultuous love-making they'd just shared.

When Alex began making love to her, Eve had made the conscious decision to no longer look back, to put the painful mistakes of the past behind her. Then, caught up in the heated assault to her senses, reality had receded, swept from her mind.

Now, with his breath warm on her forehead and his body resting on hers, she could concentrate on the total fulfillment she felt with her husband resting in her feminine warmth. She moved against him languidly, sighing with sheer bliss.

"To the victor," she murmured, her fingers playing in the silver streaks at his temples.

"I doubt if any conqueror has ever been met with such a display of hospitality," he chuckled. Eve could feel the shaking of his laugh against her spent body.

"You knew you'd win. The whole time, didn't you?"

Eve felt a momentary pang of loss as Alex levered himself up to lie on his side, his fingers tracing her curves with leisurely strokes.

"We both won," he murmured, his exploration following the slight swelling of her hips. "And no, to be perfectly honest, I wasn't nearly as confident as I seemed. I only knew how much I loved you. Nothing else in this world mattered to me if I couldn't have you by my side. Or under me," he grinned wickedly, his mustache brushing a soft path over her love-glistened body as his lips nipped at her. "Or, on top . . ."

There was still something that didn't ring true. Some little seed of doubt in the far pockets of her mind that Eve was afraid to let remain for fear it would take root, blossoming into yet another problem that might separate them once again. She took a deep breath and forced the question out into the open.

"Alex, if you felt like that in England, why didn't you come home sooner? Why did you keep silent all these months?"

He put his arm around her. "Honey, believe it or not, even the legendary Alex Steele makes a stupid mistake once in a while. As it turns out, I took some rotten advice. For a while, I was furious at you for what I thought was a deliberate abortion. But then I realized that I hadn't given you a great deal of choice with my demand that you give up your career for motherhood. I was willing to accept part of the blame. Hell, all of it, if that's what it took to get you back. I called your father and told him he'd have to replace me on the project so I could come back here and straighten out my life."

"Oh, no." Eve knew what was coming.

"Jason advised me to stay in England if I really wanted you back. He assured me you'd been having these little tantrums for years and by the time I got back, you'd welcome me with open arms."

Angry, her eyes flashed with emotion. "Dad said that? That's ridiculous! I never lost my temper in my life before I met you. I was a very calm, quiet woman. It's you who makes me crazy, Alex Steele."

"I know that now," he murmured against her lips, coaxing them open to allow entry for his tongue, successfully sidetracking her heated argument. "But, he was your father after all." He shrugged his wide shoulders.

"And the head of Olympus Studios. With a picture to complete," Eve reminded him dryly, not at all surprised by her father's maneuver. She'd learned at a very early age that business came first and foremost to Jason Meredith. Knowing that, she'd learned to love him, accepting the man as he was. Even as angry as she was right now, Eve had to admit he'd only acted in character.

"I figured that out when I got the divorce petition. By then, I had to finish out the last three weeks of shooting or everything would go down the drain. And you know what happens to hot-shot directors who blow it. What kind of future could I have offered my beautiful bride? Marriage makes a man think about things like that, you know."

"I have a job."

"Only if you win this election." His dark eyebrow arched. "Besides, do you think the taxpayers would be willing to give you a large enough raise to keep your husband in silk shirts?"

Eve laughed, running her hand down the warm skin of his chest. "Probably not. But I like you better this way."

"Honey, the feeling's mutual. But I'd wear burlap, if that's what you wanted."

Eve's eyes were as soft and inviting as a tropical lagoon.

"What I want," she whispered, her fingertips tracing the high peaks of his upper lip, "is for you to kiss me, Mr. Steele."

"With pleasure, Mrs. Steele." His lips lowered, claiming hers in a suspended, leisurely kiss.

Eventually they left the raised arbor, finding a deserted strand of beach where they let the golden warm rays of the California sun warm their bodies and the soft, foaming surf leave traces of sparkling crystals glistening on their skin. Eve thought she'd burst with sheer pleasure as Alex's tongue gathered up the tangy salt from every moist curve and hollow of her body not covered by her brief bikini.

They ran together on the hard-packed sand at the water's edge and returned home to race each other in short, frantic bursts across the heated, night-lit swimming pool. Eve laughingly joked about the exercise expunging sexual desires, but, later, neither was surprised to discover nothing of the kind had occurred.

"I enjoyed today," Alex said, holding her gaze with intimate promise. "Thank you for spending it with me."

"I enjoyed it too," she concurred breathlessly, succumbing entirely to the renewed hunger she saw in his eyes.

"You were right about the need for honest communication, Alex. I think I was just afraid of being hurt again."

"I know the feeling," he agreed. "But tonight," Alex scooped her up in his arms, "there will be other means of communication that are just as effective."

Eve looked up into his face, a small smile of enchantment on her love-softened features. "Don't tell me," she guessed on a silvery laugh. "Clark Gable and Vivien Leigh, right?"

His boisterous, wolfish grin extended right up to the

glittering black eyes as he proceeded to carry her up the sweeping curve of the long stairway. "Why, Miss Scarlett," his rough voice grated with barely constrained desire, "aren't you just the cleverest little thing?"

By the time he'd entered the master bedroom, kicking the door shut behind him, all role-playing had ceased. When Alex laid her tenderly on the wide expanse of the bed, Eve held her hands out to welcome him into her arms. Their hunger for one another was just as vital, just as alive as it had been that morning; as it had been that first night and all the lonely months in between.

"Good morning."

Eve woke to find him propped up on one elbow, gazing down at her.

"Good morning." Her lips curved into a welcoming smile. She reached up, tracing his uncompromising jawline, feeling the gritty morning beard that shadowed his skin. "I love you."

"And I love you, sweetheart." Alex's voice was vibrantly husky and betrayed obvious relief to discover that she was not going to change her mind about their decision to begin again. "What time do you have to leave for work?" he asked against her parted, responsive lips.

She rolled over, holding him down with her slim frame. "Soon." Her lips brushed the crisp, dark hairs of his chest. "But a few more minutes won't make much difference."

A deep chuckle rumbled from his chest against her lips as he willingly succumbed to her sweet seduction.

Eve had expected an argument from Barry, and was not disappointed. Seated behind her desk, her hazel eyes followed her aide as he stalked back and forth across the muted teal-blue carpet like a caged animal.

"I can't believe this!" He ceased his marching to lean over her desk, both palms flat on the glossy cherry surface. "How can you be so intelligent about everything else and be so damn stupid about your own life?" His usually smooth tones were gritty, like a harsh grade of sandpaper.

Eve shook her head in a mute gesture of regret. She appeared totally composed this morning, nothing about her poised exterior betraying the twenty-four hours of passion she'd shared with Alex. Her sleek hair was drawn into a smooth twist at the back of her neck, her cream silk blouse coordinated with the nutmeg linen suit. Tiny gold rosebud earrings graced her earlobes and on the slim third finger of her left hand, her wedding band gleamed a rich warm gold against her satiny skin. It had been months since she'd worn it and she was still experiencing a flush of pleasure whenever the glint caught her eye. Alex had slipped it on her finger the day before, his dark eyes brimming with love as he'd repeated the vows they'd almost tossed away.

Their elopement had been such a rushed affair that she and Alex had purchased the simple gold band from the first jeweler they'd spotted in Las Vegas. Monetarily, the wedding band was far from her most valuable trinket, but she owned nothing that was so treasured.

"I love him, Barry. It's that simple."

An angry flush burned his face. "Love? This is the real world, Eve, not some fanciful production from Olympus Studios. Love is not the end-all in this world." His flashing, silvery gaze narrowed. "I suppose he told you he loves you."

"That's right." Her serene eyes held a distant glint of warning as they looked up into his brooding expression. "I'm not going to discuss this any further with you, Barry. You're overstepping your bounds."

For a moment, Eve had forgotten just how long and how closely she and Barry Matthews had worked together. Now, she was about to recall that he probably knew more about her life than anyone.

"All right, if that's what you want, I'll stay out of it," he agreed, moving around to place his hands on her shoulders. "But don't forget, Eve, I'm the one who'll be around to pick up the pieces. Again."

Eve knew that Barry only had her best interests at heart. He was a close friend and she honestly dreaded the idea that this might come between them. The best way to handle the matter, she decided, was to return their conversation to their professional relationship.

She shrugged free, beginning to leaf through a stack of papers resting in her walnut "in" basket. "That's gallant of you, Barry, but it won't be necessary." She looked up, levelly meeting his gaze. "I hope you're spending as much time and mental energy worrying about my political career as you are about my personal life. That *is* your main realm of concern, remember."

"I remember, Eve," he said, settling down in a chair across from her desk. "But it's not entirely my fault, you know. You're one very special lady. Any man's bound to fall a little in love with you."

Eve's hazel eyes shadowed momentarily as they searched his handsome face for a clue as to the intent of this latest declaration. Finally, she gave up. "I still think," she said, returning her attention to the papers that had accumulated during her day off, "that you're the one who should have been the politician. I've never known you to be at a loss for the perfect words."

Barry shrugged. "I'm never one to ignore the inevitability of final returns, Eve. I enjoy working for you, although you've been giving me one hell of a headache lately. Now, here's the agenda for today. We did a bit of juggling with your schedule to fit in as many of yesterday's missed appointments as possible.'' His deep voice rolled on firmly, outlining her senatorial and campaign obligations. Eve focused her gaze on the white sheet of paper as his finger moved down it to detail her appointments. Her life was perfectly in order, she thought for a brief moment as he turned the page. At work and at home, she couldn't be happier.

The following days were busy as ever, but far more pleasant, now that she and Alex were back together. Eve insisted he return to his own work at the studios, but he still accompanied her to every appearance he could make, his company a ray of sunshine in the work-filled hours.

Eve noticed one day, as she glanced across a crowded room, that she seemed to possess the unique ability to focus only on her husband, blurring the others into a soft, hazy shadow like a camera with a short depth-of-field. At night, they'd spend the evenings quietly talking, or swimming. Or making love. In the mornings they'd share the pavement as they ran in the pearly dawn, then sit down to the light breakfast Mrs. Jacobs would have waiting. The housekeeper grumbled, with that atypical good nature Alex inspired, that Mr. Steele was trying to take over her kitchen. But Eve was still greeted with a freshly squeezed glass of orange juice each day.

''I can't believe it!'' Eve stormed through the door, slamming it behind her as she stood in the foyer, her hands curled into fists. ''For two cents I'd take this entire campaign and dump it in the trash compactor! Where it's going to belong if Peter Jordan has anything to say about it!''

Alex had come to greet her, but he stopped a few feet

short of his destination, eyeing her cautiously. The sparks were practically arcing about her slim, taut body and he could see she was trembling with rage. In her scarlet dress she looked like a brilliant flame.

"Bad day at the office?" he inquired blandly.

"*Bad day?*" Her voice rose, threatening to shatter the crystal he was holding in his hand. "Bad day?" she repeated. "It was a terrific day—if you get off on mudslinging!"

A devilish twinkle lit his dark brown eyes. "I always thought mud wrestling might be rather interesting," he drawled, "if I could get you into the ring. But mudslinging sounds untidy. You seem to have escaped unsullied, however." He cast an appreciative glance down the shimmering red shirtwaist.

"Are you laughing at me?"

A deep chortle rumbled as he closed the gap between them and pulled her into his arms, taking care not to spill the drink he was holding.

"Of course not, darling. Just trying to lighten the atmosphere a bit before dinner. I'm grilling you a steak."

Eve allowed herself the luxury of remaining in his arms. He'd been home long enough to shave, she noticed. As she buried her head in his shoulder, she inhaled the musky aroma of his after-shave along with a fresh, clean, masculine scent that had always been his alone. It acted as a tranquilizer, easing her stricken nerves, replacing the hurt and fury with love and satisfaction. The gratification a woman could receive just resting in the arms of the man she loved was better than all the Valium in all the pharmacies in the world, she decided.

"I hate him," she muttered grimly

"Jordan?"

"Who else? Mr. Let's-turn-California-back-to-the-people Jordan. As if I'd been holding the state hostage during my term!"

"I really do want to hear all about it," Alex assured her, "but for now why don't you take this drink upstairs, soothe that tense, beautiful body in the bath I've run for you, then join me out on the terrace? I'll have an effigy of the bum and dinner waiting. We can burn the effigy on the leftover coals."

Eve laughed in spite of herself. "The drink, the bath and dinner sound wonderful," she agreed. "But let's skip the effigy. If I see anything that even resembles that man right now, I'll go stark, raving mad."

She lifted her face for his kiss, closing her eyes as his lips reestablished his feelings for her. This was one of the pure pleasures of marriage, having someone who loved you and was willing to share the bad days as well as the good ones with you. Someone who was always in your corner, no questions asked. How could she have ever been so fortunate as to have a second chance with this wonderful man?

Alex's hands moved down the delicate bones of her back, patting her derriere with a friendly gesture. "Scoot," he ordered lightly, "or your bath will be cold, your champagne warm, and Lord only knows what shape your steak will be in."

Eve gave him a quick peck on the lips, then took the icy champagne that bubbled in the tulip glass and ran upstairs.

"You should have been a doctor." Eve felt years younger as she joined him out by the pool. "That was the perfect prescription."

Alex gave her a crooked grin, refilling her glass from the heavy bottle. "No, the *perfect* prescription would have been for me to join you in that bubble bath. This was only a satisfactory substitution. But I'm glad you're feeling better.''

''I am. No thanks to my unworthy opponent.''

''I almost hate to ask, since the fireworks have cooled down around here, but what did he do?''

Eve sank into a chair, crossing her long legs. She'd slipped into a pair of white jeans and a royal-blue tunic and pulled her hair back with two white combs. Alex watched her, his eyes feasting on her slender frame and delicate features. At this moment, Eve didn't look a day over seventeen. If anyone could see her like this, he thought, she'd probably never get elected. No one would believe she was old enough to vote, let alone run for office.

''You know my arts-relief bill?''

''Of course I know it. I told you it was an exceptional answer to a major problem.''

Eve smiled. He had, she remembered. Back when they were still at war. She also remembered exactly how that evening had ended.

''Well,'' she continued, reluctantly putting the erotic images of their lovemaking into a back pocket of her mind, ''the League of Women Voters has scheduled us for a debate next week.''

Alex nodded his dark head. ''I know. I've got it circled in red ink on my calendar. I have every intention of being there to lead the cheers.''

She smiled again, unable to muster up the same fury she'd felt earlier. When you were feeling so darned loved, it was hard to get incensed about anything.

''Well, I guess he decided to get in a little practice. Throwing out the first ball, so to speak. And it was a mudball. He called a press conference today, declaring that the arts-relief bill was only a ploy to put more of the taxpayers' hard-earned dollars into the greedy pockets of my father, my husband, and all my rich Hollywood friends."

Eve watched with stunned amazement as Alex's face convulsed with a sudden, violent rage. He'd drawn his body up to his full height and the power he exuded reminded Eve of those old Popeye cartoons after he'd eaten the spinach. She watched with wary fascination as Alex's hands clenched and unclenched at his sides.

"He said that? About you?" It was a softly explosive whisper, sounding far more deadly than the loudest shout would have. Eve trembled with a sudden, very real fear.

"It's just politics," she said uneasily, reaching out to touch his rigid arm. Alex was too immersed in his own exacerbation to notice.

"If he thinks he can accuse you of something like that and—"

"Alex!" She frantically searched for something to say that would erase the wrath etched onto his face. "Honey, I was the one who got carried away. It was just politics. Just the way the game's played. It wasn't meant to be taken personally." Eve's fingers clutched his arm, trying to regain his attention as she jumped up to stand in front of him.

"To most people it wouldn't be personal," Alex grated between clenched teeth. "But, damn it, you're one of the few people who really care, Eve. In your case it's goddamn personal!"

"Do you know, Alex Steele," she murmured in low, tender tones, "no one has ever loved me like you do? I can't begin to tell you how that makes me feel." Her features were glowing with pleasure as her fingers traced along his tense jawline.

"Oh Eve," he groaned, giving her a bone-crushing squeeze, "I told you I should have taken that bath with you." He gave a short, harsh laugh, then the chuckle deepened as he relaxed, able to see the humor in his behavior.

He lowered himself into a white wrought-iron glider, pulling Eve onto his lap, as he swung it gently. Taking her glass, he tipped it to his own lips.

"Much better," he said. "Now sit here and hold me down so I can't take off and kill the bastard before you tell me the rest of this sordid little political tale."

Eve lifted the glass to her own lips to take a sip before continuing. "Well, I didn't know anything about it, of course, until I was speaking at the state convention of Kiwanians. I'd opened the floor to questions and one of the reporters who'd been at Jordan's press conference asked me for a comment on his accusation."

"I'll bet it just killed the guy to have to ask that," Alex muttered acidly

She grinned. "My, you have absorbed a great deal of political savvy in the short time you've been on this campaign trail. It tickled the little squirt pink. He was there with his minicam, hoping to get a shot of Senator Steele losing her famous control and exploding in rabid, feminine passion for the six o'clock news."

"Which you didn't do."

Eve traced her fingers along the curve of his upturned lips. "No," she agreed, returning his slight smile. "I waited until I got home to treat my husband to that delightful side of my personality. Aren't you lucky to be so privileged?"

"Lucky," he agreed, lightly biting her earlobe. "What did you do?"

"I simply stated the facts." She shook her head in a slight gesture of frustration, the loose, honey silk skimming her shoulders. "The problem is that Peter Jordan was inflammatory enough to be exactly what the TV guys were looking for to liven up the campaign. My answer, on the other hand, was controlled, logical and unspectacular. It'll probably never get aired."

"Are you telling me—" Alex almost rose again, his rekindled anger sparking, and Eve flung her arms around his neck, pulling his lips down to hers.

"Alex! If I wasn't prepared to take a few hard hits, I wouldn't be out there on the field with the big guys," she assured him against his lips. "I'm used to it by now, darling. Don't worry."

"I just want to take care of you," he grumbled, his lips softening only slightly under her sustained kisses

"I never married a white knight, Alex," she answered, her tongue tracing the curve of his lips. "I've always preferred you as my dark prince."

He arched a black eyebrow rakishly. "Humphrey Bogart?"

"You're better, darling. Much, much better."

As her tongue slipped between his lips, seeking the moist, hidden interiors of his mouth, Alex's hand tunneled under the hair at the back of her neck, holding her even tighter against him. Politics, dirty tricks and everything else were forgotten as they gave themselves up to the delights their marriage had come to offer.

"Oh well," Eve laughed merrily, eyeing the charred T-bones as she poured them fresh glasses of the golden champagne. "I've always adored scrambled eggs."

# Chapter Nine

"Why, oh why, didn't I become a roller-derby queen?" Eve groaned, sinking into a chair. "Or a linebacker for the Rams? Anything less strenuous than politics."

She kicked off her high-heeled pumps, rubbing wearily at her arches.

"Barry," she said, wagging her finger at him threateningly, "you promised that the walking tour was the only thing scheduled for today. You'd better be telling the truth!"

His tanned face took on a look of feigned shock, and one hand flew to the vest of his navy-blue pinstriped suit. "Me? Lie to you?"

"Well, perhaps not lie," Eve allowed with a slight grin. "But you have been known to stretch the truth further than a six-foot rubber band."

Barry perched on the edge of her desk, the corners of his mouth lifting attractively. "You're sprung for the afternoon, kiddo," he said. "I thought you'd want some extra time carved out of your calendar to bone up for the Jordan debate."

"You are a dear." Her expression of heartfelt gratitude eased the lines of exhaustion etching her high forehead.

"You've looked a little down lately," he observed, studying her with a professional eye. "Has Steele been giving you hell about your working hours again?"

It was the first time Barry had brought up Alex since his return and his tone indicated that he still worried about the effects this reconciliation with her husband would have on her campaign.

"Everything is fine between Alex and me," Eve answered without a great deal of conviction.

She'd been struggling to balance the demands of home and career, winning some while losing others. She'd turned down a television interview program because it was taped live early on a Sunday morning, when she had promised to go to Big Bear Lake with Alex. Barry had been less than pleased about that decision.

Then there had been the dinner party Alex had thrown the night *Heaven's Rage* was released in sneak previews at selected theaters around the country. The Governor had called a special session of the legislature to address the problem of prison overcrowding and Eve had found herself stuck for five days in Sacramento. She'd arrived home in time to say goodnight to the departing guests. Alex had professed to understand, but Eve knew it had been an important evening for him, an evening when he'd wanted a wife by his side for moral support. There had been a strained air in the room after they were alone, but Eve's rueful apology had been accepted without issue.

Eve and Barry's working relationship had been going along as well as could be expected and she certainly didn't want to take the chance of disturbing things this close to the election. She needed Barry. Not with the loving intensity she needed Alex, but she was close to her aide and valued his friendship. Eve wondered briefly if either man would ever get used to the presence of the other in her life.

It was ridiculous—whenever their paths crossed, they behaved like two bulldogs fighting over a bone. And Eve did not like thinking of herself in that regard.

"You can't deny that you run down a lot easier lately," he argued. "You used to have plenty of energy until Steele moved back into your house. He's probably throwing all these dinner parties to sabotage the campaign in his own inimitable fashion."

One. One dinner party, she corrected mentally. And she'd almost missed it entirely.

"That's ridiculous," she returned with a weary sigh, too drained from the long walking trip through several neighborhoods to rise to Barry's accusation with the irritation she felt. "You're the one who's to blame, if anyone is. You've kept me going at warp speed lately."

"I seem to recall that strategy working well enough in the last campaign," he argued smoothly. "And you didn't complain then."

"I was younger," she laughed. "And back in those days I was too much in awe of you to open my mouth. Believe me, Barry Matthews, I thought very unflattering things about your propensity to load twenty-eight hours into every working day." Eve eyed him with amusement. "Have you ever considered scheduling appointments for doctors' offices? Or booking seats on airlines? You'd be a natural."

Barry grinned; the mood lightened. "Well, you only have to hold that ancient body together for two more weeks. Then if we haven't pulled it off, you'll have plenty of time for a long vacation."

A vacation, she thought as she maneuvered the car through the downtown lunch-hour traffic, was what she needed. Eve had been feeling very tired lately. While she'd always enjoyed starting her day with a jolt of adrenaline exercise supplied, yesterday it had been all she could do not to stay in bed and send Alex out to run by himself.

As she pulled into the parking lot of the medical plaza, Eve felt a twinge of guilt about keeping her appointment a secret. But Barry would worry about the campaign, if he thought she was ill. Alex, on the other hand, would insist she remain in bed and rest, forgoing all political activities. While it was nice to have two strong, capable men to worry about her, it could also become a burden when they were working at cross-purposes, Eve decided. Some vitamins, that's all she needed. By this time next week she'd be back in top form.

"When can you come in for your next appointment, dear?" The receptionist's voice seemed to come from the bottom of the sea as Eve struggled to focus her chaotic, tumbling brain on the matters at hand. Such as answering that question. She'd worry later about how to drive home without killing herself or someone else.

"What?" she asked blankly, her eyes attempting to focus on the grandmotherly woman.

"Your next appointment. Four weeks," she announced. "What day is convenient, Mrs. Steele?" Busy fingers flipped through the large desk appointment book, running down the columns as she looked up expectantly for Eve's answer.

"I'll call you," Eve managed to get out, anxious to leave.

She walked out to the car, her legs feeling as if they were in danger of buckling under her. She felt like she'd just been kicked by a horse, a very big one. The rumbling in her stomach reminded her that she'd forgotten to eat lunch and she ran her palms over the front of her linen skirt, staring blankly at the smooth, slim lines of her body.

When Eve arrived home, her whirling mind had still not managed to sort its way through the unexpected shock of her pregnancy. It was too soon. She and Alex had managed to establish a workable marriage, but it was still so fragile. She knew they'd both been walking about the house on eggshells, trying to keep from giving each other cause to regret this reconciliation.

Her overcharged brain filled with images of Alex's face when she had presented him with the news of her first pregnancy. While he said that he'd always wanted their child, he'd stood horribly still in the doorway of that wretched motel room, staring at her with—what? Shock? Anger? Panic? Eve shook her head, unable to pinpoint his exact, instantaneous response. Alex would be able to, she knew. He was in the business of directing such scenes. But she knew that whatever he'd been thinking at that moment, he hadn't been thrilled.

As if in a trance, she made her way up the curving staircase, forgetting even to take off her shoes as she lay back on the bed, her arms folded under her head as she began a contemplative study of the ceiling.

Hours later, she had paced a worn path in the Aubusson carpet and her nail polish had been chewed off in intense concentration while Eve had made a decision. She loved Alex, and she had given this marriage a second chance because she believed Alex loved her. No, she mused, she *knew* he loved her. The trick was telling the man a little more subtly this time. Eve smiled a feminine smile as she moved to the bedside phone, punching seven digits with renewed energy.

"Hello."

The voice which answered the private number sounded

tired and drained. Eve refused to let his fatigue serve as an excuse to put her news off for another day.

"Hi," she said with an overabundance of cheer. "I thought I'd call and see how long you're going to be working."

"Oh, honey." The harshness softened and Alex's voice took on the soft brogue that could pull at her heartstrings like a virtuoso harpist. "Did we have something planned?"

"No. I was planning an intimate little supper at home. How was your day? Will you be able to get away soon?"

"The day was a total wash," he answered on a deep breath. "Although it sounds as if you may be able to salvage it for me. How intimate is this little supper going to be?"

"Mrs. Jacobs is back visiting in Glendale and I seem to have this big, lonely house all to myself."

"That intimate, huh?" Alex laughed appreciatively. "I think, Mrs. Steele, that you've saved the day."

"I'm so glad," Eve murmured. "Who was foolhardy enough to get in your way this time?" Eve knew that Alex was used to receiving carte blanche for everything in his life. He insisted on total control and, while he might have been willing to relinquish the iron hand at home, she knew he still wielded it at the studio.

"It's just been one of those days," he muttered. "First, David Marshall showed up, like the specter of death from some old Ingmar Bergman movie. Black and white. The guy would never rate Technicolor."

"All tax accountants are supposed to look like the doorman at the House of Usher," she remarked, thinking that David Marshall's countenance was a great deal like that of a manic-depressive bloodhound. One who'd gotten stuck on the downward swing. "What jolly news did he bring you?"

"We may be losing the tax shelter from advertising expenses," he muttered. "If the investors get back their original expense, plus twelve percent, the IRS will probably consider it a loan, and disallow the tax deduction. If they keep tightening the screws on deductions, we'll have a harder time finding investors."

It seemed a shame to her that an artistic man like Alex would have to become so involved in the murky, financial dealings of the movie business. Eve sighed, wishing idly for the good old days, even before her time, when the studios produced, the directors directed, the actors played their parts and long lines extended on the sidewalks outside the huge, elaborate theaters. When the dollars seemed to come from some gigantic money-making machine, stimulated by a constant stream of successful, profit-producing movies. Now, more time seemed to be spent deciding who was going to get what percentage of the gross profits before the screenplay had even rolled from the typewriter.

"You'll never have a problem," she assured him. "People will stand in line to get a piece of the action on any project you direct, Alex."

"Spoken like a faithful wife," he chuckled. "In fact, give me forty minutes and I'll be home to show my appreciation for your support."

"Try thirty," she suggested with warm invitation. "This place is getting lonelier and lonelier."

"Twenty-five and you've got yourself a deal."

Eve prepared well and an exotic cloud of perfume was the first thing Alex noticed when he entered the dining room in search of her. The fresh top note immediately gave way to the flowery middle scent of roses, jasmine, acacia and orange blossoms. Then, just as his olfactory sense was getting used to the complex floral base, like a blow from behind, the musk and amber crept around his head, dense, rich and tenacious. He was enveloped in its seductive mist and he turned slowly, eyeing the alluring woman poised in the doorway.

Eve almost laughed aloud, watching his jaw drop slightly and his dark eyes take on a rapid-fire blinking motion. She crossed the room in a long glide, closing in on him like a huntress, her hips moving gracefully. Her slender body was clad in a silk crepe dress the color of rich country cream. Halter style, it dipped to a low, low waist in back, displaying her smooth, tawny skin. The front was also slit to the waist, teasing the eye with visual promise. The dress clung seductively, hugging and caressing her curves like a lover's caress as it slid over her hips to flare slightly about the knees, enhancing the long length of shapely calves.

She placed her fingers on his chest as he stood like a statue. Eve could feel the rapid beat of his heart under her hands as they moved across his body. Alex moved as if in slow motion, his eyes wide as he placed his hands on either side of the smooth indentation of her waist. When his hands moved to her back, he could feel the satiny smoothness of her perfumed skin.

Eve lifted her head and smiled at him, bringing his attention to the splendid column of her throat. As his lips pressed against the fragrant pulse spot, her hands moved up his arms to play in the waves of jet and silver hair. The action curved her hips into him and Alex stared into her sultry emerald eyes, wondering just where this alluring enchantress had come from.

He'd known Eve at her most appealing—a woman who could meet him at any and all heights of lovemaking—but he'd never experienced such a performance as the one she was giving right now. Enticing, beguiling, she was ensnaring him in a sensual trap as old as time. Before his eyes she'd become Jezebel, Salome, Delilah, and he was as drawn to her as if she were a mythical siren and he a bewitched sailor.

The tip of her tongue tasted him, moving along his jawline. The sound of it brushing against the nighttime stubble of beard seemed to echo in his ears, along with the intense throbbing of his own blood. Alex tried to capture her stroking lips with his own, but Eve turned her head, eluding his questing mouth as she touched the soft skin behind his ear with a silky touch, pressing little intoxicating kisses around his earlobe before exploring the deep inner shell.

Strange heats burst inside him, little fires that sparked all his nerve endings. His hands cupped the soft curve of her hips, urging her against him, but Eve seemed determined to set the pace and gave him a sweet smile as she pulled slightly away, denying him the warmth of her body.

Her finger moved to his shirt, unbuttoning it with slow, deliberate movements. Then she tugged, pulling it loose from his slacks, and pulled the silk slowly off his body until it lay at their feet. Her hands slid in sensuous exploration against the hard wall of his chest, her lips following the teasing path through the thick black carpeting of hair.

Then she lifted her head, backing away a few inches once again. With remarkable control, she reached up to the back of her neck, a small smile of enchantment touching her lips. Alex's attention was drawn to the languid gesture with which she unfastened the halter, allowing the top of her dress to fall to her waist. The blood glowed warmly beneath her silken skin and as his eyes raked over her, the raw hunger burned through his veins. With a sweeping surge of male passion, Alex groaned, dragging her into the feverish heat of his body. Eve found herself helplessly swept up into the seductive, sexual atmosphere she'd set about creating. His lips moved over her face, tasting her, the rough stubble grating against her cheeks and lips.

He moved her hips in deliberate circles as he ground her body against him and when Eve's arms looped about his waist, holding him even tighter, his hands traveled seductively under her dress, his fingers climbing up her nylon-clad thigh. She gave a whisper of pleasure against his ravaging lips, her head thrown back in unconscious rapture. His strong fingers probing at her heated feminine core were not to be denied and she cried out, turning her head into his shoulder, her muffled gasps disappearing into his glistening skin as he tore the filmy webbing, thrusting into the moist, secret recesses. Eve moved against the marauding strokes, her head swimming and her legs weakening so she could only cling to the solid strength of his shoulders as he held her on her feet, the treacherous hands bringing her to the very edge of a dangerous, erotic abyss.

Eve wanted him to stop so she could regain control. After all, she'd been the one seducing him. On the other hand, if he did cease, she thought she might very well die of desire. The caressing, probing fingers drew a moan of joyful ecstasy as she reached for him without restraint, wishing to bring him to the same heights to which he was bringing her.

Finally, when they'd both wrung the eager passion into wild longing, the atmosphere explosive with unleashed savagery, Alex dragged his mouth from hers, taking deep breaths.

"I don't know what you planned to accomplish, Eve," he gasped, the sound harsh and labored as if he'd just finished running a marathon, "but I can't wait for you another minute."

"I planned," she said, her voice half honey and half smoke, "to invite the incredibly sexy Alex Steele to ravish his pregnant wife."

Alex's gaze moved over her softened features, searching out the truth of her overwhelming statement. He wanted to burst with expanded joy. "Pregnant? You're going to have my baby? Are you sure?"

"I'm sure," she murmured, her palms on either side of his astonished, ecstatic face. "Dr. Sebastian was also surprised, by the way." Eve's smile was as warm and loving as any a woman ever shared with a man. "But of course, he doesn't realize what an incredibly virile man I'm married to. Speaking of which . . ."

Alex needed no further invitation, his cry of acceptance lost as he scooped her up, crushing her against his bare chest as he carried her up the stairs to the bedroom, where his hands practically ripped the remaining clothes off their heated bodies.

With a tenderness that belied his hunger, he slipped deliciously into her, treating her as if she were a piece of delicate, hand-blown crystal. Eve lifted her hips, meeting him with an all-consuming eagerness.

"Oh Alex . . ." Her teeth closed in agonized torment on the glistening skin of his shoulder.

Alex established a slow, devastating rhythm that allowed him absolute control as she twisted in his arms, the last remaining vestiges of coherent thought and reserve vanishing. Consumed with a desperate, feminine need, Eve twisted her legs about his narrow hips, her body pleading for an end to the sweet, savage torment.

"Please, Alex." One silken leg covered his as she attempted to move him onto his back so she could regain the initiative that he'd so effectively stolen from her. But he held her, not wavering from his intended mastery of the situation.

With long, languid strokes, he succeeded in bringing Eve to the very brink of ecstasy, each time backing down before she could tumble over the edge.

"I've wanted you since the moment I saw you," he whispered against her lips, his tongue plundering the honey behind her teeth. "But you've become an obsession, Eve. I want you more every day. I'll never get enough of you." The force of his declaration was echoed by his body as he surged against her, claiming her irrevocably.

"You have me," she cried, giving up on her attempts to recapture any control over his lovemaking. She rode the spiraling waves of desire, desperate for fulfillment of the pulsating ache he'd created in every nerve of her body.

"I need more, Eve. I need you to want me just as badly."

"My God, Alex, I need you. Can't you tell? I love you. There's never been anyone else like you . . ."

Her fingers tangled in his hair, her mouth eating into his as their warm breath mingled. "Oh Alex," she cried in hoarse pleas for fulfillment. "Please, I think I'm going to explode . . ."

There was an incredible pressure building up within her and Eve felt the heat swelling and cascading with mysterious ferocity as she lost the last modicum of control over her shaking limbs. Alex began to move against her in that wild, wonderous rhythm, as if his own passion had suddenly burst its bonds of constraint.

"Alex!"

"Yes, Eve. Yes, honey. Now . . ."

The darkness seemed to burst and glow with a fire as they clung together, sensation after sensation thrusting them at long last over the edge of the precipice in a full, joyous climax that sent them spinning, until ultimately reaching safe ground once more, still wrapped in each other's arms. They remained that way for a long time, their hands languidly stroking love-warmed flesh. Alex was the first to break the golden silence.

"If you wanted to convince me that pregnant ladies are sexy, well, you sure as hell put forth a good case, sweetheart." His eyes danced with a devilish gleam. "If that's what I have to look forward to, I think we ought to give serious consideration to keeping you pregnant from now on."

Her fingers played with his thick mustache. He looked so very pleased with himself, Eve thought with a bit of feminine amusement. If a man could resemble a strutting peacock while sprawled naked on a satin comforter, Alex was pulling it off. She traced the uplifted line of his lips.

"You don't mind, then?"

Ebony brows lifted high on his forehead. "Mind? I think it's the best news I've ever had. I've already told you how I felt about you having my child . . ." His hooded eyes narrowed slightly as they scanned her face, his expression suddenly serious. "Are you sure *you* don't mind?"

"I'm thrilled," she answered honestly. She cuddled up against him, fitting the soft contours of her body to his hard length. "It was wonderful enough to be given a fresh start to our marriage, Alex. To have a second chance for a child is almost a miracle." Her fingers laced together in his hair, as she rained a light shower of kisses over his strangely somber features. "Why would I feel anything but ecstatic?"

"Well, the timing isn't perfect."

"Timing?" Eve answered him absently, her attention directed to nibbling on his earlobe.

"Isn't it going to be hard for the party to come up with another candidate this close to the election?"

At first the words flew right over the top of her head, busy as she was creating a trail of soft kisses down his dark tanned throat. Then, as the carefully issued question took hold, Eve slowly raised her head.

"What do you mean? I'm the candidate, Alex. Nothing's changed there."

"Nothing's changed?" He pushed himself into a sitting position, the gesture effectively shaking her from him. He crossed his arms over his naked chest and Eve noted his disgruntled surprise with apprehension. "I'd say a hell of a lot has changed, Eve. You're going to be a mother."

Eve sat up as well, gathering the sheet up against her. Her voice stayed incredibly calm, her political training overcoming her growing fear.

"And you're going to be a father, Alex. But I'm not asking you to give up directing," she replied.

"That's different and you damn well know it," he gritted between tightly clenched teeth. "Don't go pulling any of your slick debating tricks on me, Senator. I'm not as easily sidetracked as your usual opponent."

Eve felt like she was walking through a dark, hostile valley as she tried to figure a way to salvage this increasingly perilous conversation. They were back to that—opponents in an age-old war of the sexes.

"Alex," she said softly, reaching a hand out to rest on his thigh, "women have babies every day and don't stop work. Even your mother. You told me she had eight children, and she kept working."

"You're doing it again," he complained, spearing her with a gaze as black as pitch. "You're confusing the issue. She's a strong, healthy woman, made for bearing children. You've already proven that you're far more delicate. This time we're going to do it right, Eve. You're going to do nothing but rest until the baby's born. Then we'll talk about whether or not you need anything besides your husband and child to satisfy you."

Eve pushed back her tumbled hair, ignoring the sheet, which fell down to her waist. She stared at him in a paralyzing moment of insight, unable to believe this was the same Alex Steele she thought she'd come to know.

"You make it sound as if we're two different breeds," She tilted her chin stubbornly, livid spots of color in her cheeks a distinct contrast to the unusual pallor of her skin. "I'm perfectly capable of bearing a child just as well as the next woman, Alex Steele. I don't need to be wrapped in cellophane and put away on a damn shelf for the next seven months!"

Alex was upset now, his temples pounding thickly, his throat tight. Disbelief and rage mingled as he struggled to comprehend what he saw as Eve's displaced sense of priorities. His despair burned the last vestige of logic and reason from his mind as he sharpened his tongue for the confrontation.

"You've already proven how capable you are of carrying a baby, Eve. If you hadn't been so damn insistent on keeping your senate seat, we might not have lost one child. How many times are you going to tempt fate for your own selfish reasons?"

His words came at her like bullets and Eve struck out in blind desperation, staring in shock at the vivid, white imprint on his dark skin. She'd only hit one person in her life before this and that, too, had been Alex, during their argument in Mexico. The sharp crack of her palm against his face was followed by a stunned silence and both pairs of eyes moved to her uplifted hand.

"I guess that's my answer." Alex could feel all the will

drain out of him and spoke with a despair he made no attempt to conceal. Pushing himself slowly from the bed, he bent to gather up the strewn items of his clothing.

"What are you doing?" Eve was on her knees on the tangled sheets, reaching out for him, unwilling to believe that he would let everything end this way. Not again, her mind and heart cried out. Oh dear God, not again!

"I think this is where I came in." There was a tired droop to his shoulders as he dressed, the powerful physique seeming less authoritative than she'd ever seen it. His tone was heavy with resignation. "I love you, Eve, more than anything in the world. But you're asking too much. You want everything from life. I thought my love would be enough for you, but I see now it's not."

"We agreed that I had my own career, Alex. I don't understand what's wrong."

He eyed her with gentle disapproval, the silent appraisal going on for what seemed to Eve like an eternity. There was far more sorrow than fury in his unguarded dark eyes and she wished she could think of one thing that would put a stop to this before they destroyed what they'd worked so hard to rebuild.

"When we agreed to that, Eve, you told me we couldn't count on children. I understood how difficult that was going to be for you. So," he lifted his shoulders in a weary shrug, "I was willing to agree to your work so you could fill the void in your life. But now you don't need it any longer. Don't you see? You'll have a family. A husband and child who love you."

"People love their pets, too, Alex. But if you cage a pet in order to keep it near you, it will run away at the first opportunity," Eve stated softly. "There's room in my life for both a home and a career, Alex. Please don't try to chain me down like this."

The pain in his gaze tore her heart to shreds and Eve knew she'd lost the argument. And her husband. When he spoke, there was a final, implacable note in his voice.

"I'm sorry you consider my love a chain, Eve. I never meant it to be like that. I only wanted to make you happy."

He gave her one long, last look before leaving the room. Eve ran to the top of the stairs, her knuckles white as she gripped the carved mahogany railing, watching him descend without a backward glance.

# Chapter Ten

"Well, congratulations, Senator Steele." Barry turned off the engine of the car as he parked in the driveway outside Eve's home. "You did it."

"*We* did it," she corrected softly, staring out into the blackness of the early morning. There was a new moon and the only illumination was the muted shades of the landscape lights adorning her front yard, casting long shadows across the lawn. "You know I couldn't have done it without you, Barry. Again."

He put his hand gently on her shoulder, his fingers massaging with soothing strokes. "Let's just say we make a great team, Eve, and not argue over who needs whom the most."

"Agreed."

"You put on a great show tonight. Sometimes I think you should have listened to your father."

She turned from her intense scrutiny of the darkness outside the car to Barry's inscrutable face.

"What do you mean by that?"

"I mean that you probably could have been one hell of an actress. When Jordan came on the tube with his concession speech, the entire crowd thought you were ecstatic with your victory. But we know better, don't we?"

"I know you don't like Alex, Barry, so, I really don't want to talk about him with you. It's still too painful."

"I like him."

"What?" Eve was stunned. "Since when? You two were at sword points for the past two months. You were both driving me crazy!"

"I admire the guy, Eve. Who wouldn't? He knows exactly what he wants out of life and goes after it full steam ahead. I just wasn't sure he was good for you. Alex has the need to control everyone around him and I didn't want to see you stuck under his thumb. I'm fond of you, Eve. Hell, more than that and you know it. Given a little encouragement, who knows . . ." His voice drifted off, and she felt a cool sense of relief that he wasn't going to follow up on that particular topic.

"Anyway," he continued, his crooked smile letting her know he understood, "I was afraid you might be willing to give up your career for him. You've got too many of your own talents and ambitions, honey, to end up playing an adoring Annette to his Frankie. That sorta stuff made cute movies, but it doesn't work in real life, kiddo."

"Katherine Hepburn to his Cary Grant," she murmured, thinking back to Alex's assertion that first evening.

"What?" Barry missed her soft correction.

"Nothing. You have to admit that in the long run, Alex probably helped the campaign more than anything else. Even to covering our breakup with that story."

"Yeah. I meant to ask you about that." Barry's eyes narrowed thoughtfully. "What was all that stuff about a family emergency taking him to Ireland? It's hard to think of the great Alex Steele living any type of normal childhood existence. Have you ever met them?"

Eve shook her head. "I don't know if there's any truth to the story or not. I didn't even know his family existed until a few weeks ago. Alex was an expert at not letting people get close to him, but I think his mother made far more of an impression on him than he'd be willing to admit."

"He's a tough nut to crack, all right," Barry agreed. "But I'll give him credit for having some warped code of honor. He could have gotten his way by announcing your latest separation and the reason for it. I'm not sure a woman who considers her career more important than a family could win many votes."

"Not you too!" Eve's eyes flashed with a sudden anger as she turned in her seat toward him. "I thought you were on my side in all this!"

Barry held up his hands in a gesture of apology. "Hey, I am. I was just saying that Steele could have made it look that way if he'd wanted to." His gaze grew thoughtful. "I wonder why he didn't?"

Eve shook her head, unable to answer. She'd asked herself that question at least once a day for the past two weeks, warily awaiting Alex's bomb that would effectively blow her campaign to smithereens. All's fair in love and war, he'd threatened her. The only explanation she'd been able to come up with when everything remained ominously silent on the Ireland front was that Alex no longer loved her enough to fight for her. Instead of experiencing relief at that thought, she'd suffered a new pain, far worse than the original.

She'd fought a long and tedious battle to maintain her senate seat, something she'd wanted with her entire heart. But when the channel seven news team projected her victory, shortly after three A.M. she discovered it was a bittersweet victory. While she'd won the battle, she'd lost the war. And the man she loved.

"You look beat," Barry broke into her unhappy thoughts. "You'd better go upstairs and get to bed. Remember, Senator, you're sleeping for two these days."

"Thank you, Barry."

He flashed her a look of honest surprise as she leaned forward and kissed him lightly on the cheek. "For what?"

"For everything. Here I am, wallowing in self-pity, when I'm lucky enough to have you for a friend."

For once Barry seemed to lack the ability to come up with the appropriate response. He was silent, holding her hand as he walked her to the door.

"Eve?" he offered, as if it were an afterthought. "I hope you'll always consider me your friend."

Eve searched the softened planes of the handsome face in the amber glow of the porch light. He looked decidedly troubled about something. It struck her that neither one of them looked as if they'd ended the campaign on the winning side.

"Of course I will."

He nodded gravely, his gray eyes shadowed to a deep smoke. "I sure hope so," he muttered, jamming his hands into his pockets and turning away.

The phone rang as she entered the living room, effectively halting her pensive thoughts.

"Eve, is that you?"

"Of course, Dad. Who would you expect to be answering my phone at this hour?" The weary voice sounded nothing like her own.

"We must have a bad connection here, honey. I can hardly hear you!" Jason Meredith raised his own voice considerably, as if somehow that would solve the problem.

"We tried to call you at the hotel, Eve, but the phone was busy all evening. Congratulations, darling! I'm sorry I wasn't there with you."

Eve had been so busy longing for Alex's presence, watching the doorway in the vain hope that he'd appear, that she hadn't paid any attention to her father's absence. "That's okay, Dad. I'm sure you were busy."

"You could say that again. I'm in Las Vegas."

"How nice." That certainly wasn't unusual. How odd it was that the world had kept on turning, even as hers had been tipped upside down.

"I'll be back in three, maybe four days."

"Dad, surely this conversation can wait until later in the day."

"Sure, honey. I know you're probably bushed. I just wanted to tell you that I'm bringing your new stepmother back with me."

That did it. His words cut instantly through her lassitude like a hot knife through butter.

"Stepmother! Who?"

"Nat, of course. Who did you expect?"

Eve sank down into a chair behind a small antique desk. "Dad, I've always really liked Natalie. I'm just a little surprised that you're married," she admitted honestly.

"Hell, honey, how do you think I feel? But I just couldn't get rid of this one. Seems the gal actually loves me."

"I'm happy for you dad," she murmured, trying her best to mean it. Right now, the thought of marriage—anyone's marriage—was a little hard to handle.

"Do you know what she did?" The booming voice echoed in her ear and Eve held the receiver a little away from her.

"Of course I don't."

"Damn fool woman turned down Anna Karenina. Can you believe that?"

Eve's eyebrows rose. She might not be interested in a movie career herself, but she knew a great deal about the business. And she knew that the role of Anna would be a good one. It could very well earn an Oscar for the young actress fortunate enough to be given the part. "She did that? Why?"

"That's what I asked her. Guess what her answer was?"

"Dad," Eve replied with forced patience, "how could I possibly know?"

"Said the part would involve too many months on location and she didn't want to leave me for that long. Silly damn woman seems to think I need looking after." Jason Meredith's voice grew thick with unbridled emotion, the tone sounding forced and unusually husky. "Imagine that. Turned down the best damn part since *The French Lieutenant's Woman*. Hell, probably the best since Scarlett O'Hara! For an obstreperous old man . . . Here, I'll let you talk to the bride."

"Eve?" Natalie's soft, delicate voice came over the line in place of her father's bass drumrolls and Eve could sense her nervousness. "Congratulations on your reelection."

"It's you who deserves the congratulations," Eve replied, meaning every word. "Although it's best wishes for the bride, isn't it?"

"You don't mind?"

"Mind? I think it's wonderful. And if Dad gives you one moment's trouble, I'll personally come over and threaten mayhem." Eve laughed lightly, feeling somewhat buoyed by the love this oddly matched couple had found. "Natalie, I'm thrilled. But don't expect me to call you Mommy."

"You're a wonderful person, Eve. And I want you to know that you won't be dragged to any more parties you don't want to attend. Now that I'm Jason's wife, I'll love being his hostess." Natalie's soft voice took on a slight tremor. "It was only that I felt like just another one of his women passing through. I couldn't stand the way everyone looked at us, thinking I was only after what he could do for my career. I only wanted to love him and take care of him."

"You're one in a million, Nat," Eve said sincerely. "And I'm glad Dad was smart enough to recognize it. I did long ago. I wish you both a glorious marriage."

"Thanks. If we can be half as happy as you and Alex, I'll be perfectly content."

Alex. Eve wondered what Natalie would think if she were to divulge the state of that relationship. But no, this was the young woman's happiest day. She wasn't about to destroy it with her own problems.

"Nat, I've got to go—" Eve broke off softly, trying to ease out of a conversation that was beginning to renew the ache in her chest.

"Of course. Take care, Eve."

"You too, Nat. I'll see you when you get back."

Eve replaced the receiver gently on its cradle and stared at it for a very long time. Suddenly, her mind lit with a vivid clarity, like the water in a stream fed from melting snows. For the first time, everything seemed to make sense. All the shattered pieces of her life seemed to be lying there in front of her, waiting for her to fit them back together into a workable whole. Reaching into the desk drawer, she pulled out a sheet of stationery and a pen.

An hour later, the polished oak floor was covered with crumpled pieces of false starts, but finally Eve rose from the desk, satisfied. She rubbed the back of her neck wearily, glancing at the grandfather clock on the far wall. The room was bathed in a rose and golden glow and she realized that dawn was just over the horizon.

Eve knew she'd need her rest for what was coming. But a brief, relaxing dip in the pool while she watched the sun rise could only help her sleep. She opened the French doors, stopping in her tracks when she looked toward the pool.

"What are you doing here?"

Alex saw her suddenly ashen expression as she swayed in the doorway and was by her side, catching her as she almost fainted from a combination of shock and exhaustion.

"Waiting for you. Matthews promised to bring you home as soon as the results were announced. Congratulations, by the way. I voted for you."

It was too much for Eve's whirling mind to assimilate at one time. Her hands still clung to his shoulders as he lowered her into a lounge chair. Moving aside her legs, Alex sat on the edge, looking at her with obvious concern.

"Are you all right? Do you need a doctor?"

Her fingers dug into the skin of his shoulders under the soft leather jacket. "I'm fine. I was just surprised to see you, that's all." Her smooth brow furrowed, trying to remember what he'd just said.

"Barry knew you'd be here?"

"He did. He also told me he thought you'd be up to handling the surprise." His lips drew into a firm line. "I admire the guy's political expertise, Eve, but I sure as hell don't think he knows much about you. That's why I wanted to wait and see you alone, here. I was afraid something like this might happen." He gave her a tentative smile. "I wasn't certain you'd be willing to talk to me. I didn't want to take unfair advantage by cornering you in public in case you felt like slugging me again."

She reached out, running a trembling palm against his cheek. "I don't know what made me do that. I'm usually quite controlled."

"Except with me." His dark eyes held a glimmer of laughter.

Eve allowed herself a slight smile. "Except with you," she agreed, not taking her eyes from his dancing jet gaze. Then something else occurred to her.

"Did you say you voted for me?"

Alex's ebony hair was sparked with the golden glow of the rising sun as he nodded. It struck her suddenly that her dark, fallen angel appeared terribly incongruous wearing a halo, and she laughed, a light, breathless laughter born of overwhelming nervousness. What was he doing here?

"Of course I did. As a man in love, I may be an idiot, but as an informed voter, I always select the best man for the job. Or, in this case, woman."

"But if I'd lost, there would have been nothing standing in our way."

Alex held both her hands as his long fingers played with the simple golden band adorning her left hand.

"There would have been a hell of a lot standing in our way, Eve. The first being that you'd never believe I really wanted you to win. I was a nervous wreck waiting for the final returns tonight. It was incredibly important to me that you knew I wanted you back—with your career."

"Why?"

"Because I wanted to prove that I loved you enough to unfasten the chains. You were right, Eve. I was being selfish."

She shook her head. "No, you weren't. You were right, Alex. I was the one who was being selfish. I wanted everything my way."

"Damn it, woman, will you quit trying to steal my

apology? I've been rehearsing this scene for days." The smile in his deep voice assured her that he wasn't actually angry. Then he continued seriously, "I only wanted a wife on my own terms. I kept thinking of you as Eve, the wife. Or Eve, the mother. Never Eve, the gorgeous, bright, loving individual I'd fallen head over heels for. I love you, Senator Steele. And, if you'll give a chauvinistic, nineteenth-century Irish idiot one more try, I promise not to blow it this time."

Eve stared at him, a glimmer of amusement in her hazel eyes. "Oh Alex, I can't believe this!"

"I'm not acting, Eve. Believe me." His harshly hewn features took on an expression of barely suppressed desperation and Eve flung her arms around him, pressing a forceful kiss on his lips. "Wait a minute." She left the chair to run back into the house. Returning a moment later, she waved the paper she'd struggled over. "Read this," she instructed, shoving it into his hands.

Eve watched the waves of emotion wash over his dark face. First curiosity, then surprise, then an expression so soft, so revealing, it was all she could do to keep from throwing herself into Alex's arms to spend the rest of the morning proving her words to him.

He raised hesitant eyes to her, the disbelief fading as he saw her expression. "You were going to do this?"

"I was."

"Why?"

"I think that's fairly obvious."

His dark appraisal sharpened, sweeping down her still-slender body. "There's no problem with the baby, is there?"

"Of course not," Eve quickly reassured him, effectively banishing the worry that had shown on his strong features.

"Then I don't understand."

"I love you, Alex. More than anyone or anything in this entire world. You said you couldn't change the way you were. You also told me I couldn't have you and my career." She shrugged and gave him the beautiful smile of a woman confortable with her decision. "Anyone can have a career. A life with Alex Steele might not be the most tranquil way to spend my days, but I'm willing to chance it if you are." Her fingertips stroked his high-planed cheekbone.

Alex swept her into an embrace so strong, so powerful, that for a long moment, as his lips covered hers and drank with a desperate, thirsty greed, she was afraid all her ribs would be broken, after which she'd surely suffocate. But he loosened his hold at the same time he dragged his mouth from hers. His lips pressed against the pulsebeat in her temple as his warm breath fanned her hair.

"God, how I adore you."

"And I love you, darling. With my whole heart and soul."

"And you're actually willing to let me be the boss of this family once in a while?"

She leaned her head back to look into his happy face. "I suppose so," she sighed with exaggerated acceptance, "if that's what it takes to keep the legendary director satisfied."

"Good. I'm glad we've finally gotten that settled. Now, for my first order—"

"Pretty fast with the proclamations, aren't you, Mr. Steele?"

"Just in time, apparently," he stated, tearing up the paper she'd labored over.

"Alex! I don't have a copy of that." Eve reached out, trying to catch the pieces as they drifted to the ground like snowflakes.

"Good. Because as a citizen of this state, I would feel cheated if the duly reelected senator resigned her seat just to stay home and play house with her husband."

"That's the citizen talking," she pointed out. "What about the husband?"

"He'd like to invite his wife to take a few days' vacation with him before she returns to the salt mines."

"It sounds wonderful." Eve sighed happily, moving to settle more comfortably in his arms. "Where shall we go?"

Alex's chin was on the top of her head and Eve couldn't see his expression. "I was thinking of Belfast." His bland admission caused Eve's heart to take wing.

"Are you going to introduce me to your family?"

"I think it's high time," he stated with casual indifference. "Although we'll probably end up with a lot of time to ourselves. It seems that Ma has used all that money I've been sending home to expand the bakery. She's now supplying soda bread to half the Continent with her own mail-order business. She probably won't have much time for entertaining a pair of old married folks."

A twinkling light brightened Eve's eyes. "Is this the lady you were so eager to leave so she could relax and give up the heavy burdens of the marketplace?"

There was a good-natured reluctance to his answer. "Could be," he admitted.

"And is this the same lady who only worked because she had all those hungry mouths to feed? Who longed for the life of comfortable leisure you offered me?"

"Could be." Attractive lines fanned outward from the corners of his eyes. "But it only proves I was right about one thing."

"And that is?" Her own bright eyes were spiked with shared laughter. At this moment, Eve didn't know whom she loved more; Alex for caring enough to examine his feelings and trying to change, or his mother for helping him understand that even a woman very much in love with a man could need to feel a sense of her own worth.

He shrugged. "Women. Who can figure 'em? I'm still adjusting to the fact that I just voted for one."

"In case you've forgotten, Alex Steele, you made a few campaign promises of your own." Her hands rubbed ever-widening circles on his chest.

"I did?" One ebony brow arched with devilish amusement. "What promises were those?"

Eve began deliberately unbuttoning his shirt. "You promised to woo me, win me and make mad, passionate love to me," she reminded him as she moved to explore his bared skin.

"You're right," Alex agreed readily. She caught her breath as his hand moved over her stomach, his palm stroking the hidden spot where their child rested. "Which promise shall I begin with?"

"Any." Eve settled into his embrace, feeling like a winner for the first time since the prediction had been announced hours ago. "All," she decided as his lips reestablished familiarity with her satiny skin, his clever hands sending their clothing scattering across the poolside terrace.

He chuckled. "I don't know—I've never heard of anyone keeping every one of his campaign promises."

"Who knows," Eve's answering laugh was a throaty, husky sound as she rained light kisses over his rugged features. "You might just start a trend the rest of us will have to follow. It could do wonders for the American political system."

"Then you're in luck, Mrs. Steele," he replied with a lascivious, teasing grin.

"I am?" Eve inquired innocently.

"Yes. It just so happens that your husband is a very patriotic fellow."

Alex rolled over to blanket her with his solid strength, his lips covering hers in a fervent pledge that would endure a lifetime.